RONAN

BRIDGE

AMULET BOOKS

NEW YORK

BOYLE

AND THE

OF RIDDLES

THOMAS LENNON

·ILLUSTRATED BY JOHN HENDRIX·

Cataloging-in-Publication Data has been applied for and may be obtained from the Library of Congress.

ISBN 978-1-4197-3491-5
U.K. paperback ISBN 978-1-4197-3905-7
Special edition ISBN 978-1-4197-3916-3

TEXT COPYRIGHT © 2019 THOMAS LENNON
ILLUSTRATIONS COPYRIGHT © 2019 JOHN HENDRIX
BOOK DESIGN BY CHAD W. BECKERMAN

Printed and bound in U.S.A.
10 9 8 7 6 5 4 3 2 1

Amulet Books are available at special discounts when purchased in quantity for premiums and promotions as well as fundraising or educational use. Special editions can also be created to specification. For details, contact specialsales@abramsbooks.com or the address below.

Amulet Books® is a registered trademark of Harry N. Abrams, Inc.

ABRAMS The Art of Books
195 Broadway, New York, NY 10007
abramsbooks.com

For Oliver

OFFICE OF FINBAR DOWD
Deputy Commissioner
Special Unit of Tir Na Nog
Collins House, Killarney
Kerry, Ireland

23 June

TO: Trainees of the Special Unit

FROM: Office of the Deputy Commissioner

POLITE WARNING!

A box containing this diary was mailed to the Galway office of the garda by Lieutenant Ronan Boyle. The package was 18 kilograms (40 pounds) in weight and poorly taped together.

Boyle's files span several years and conclude with his disappearance—seven Wednesdays ago. This document is available via Ireland's 1997 Freedom of Information Act. The commissioner hopes that you might glean some experience from these pages and avoid Boyle's fate, which seems nasty. If Boyle is not deceased, he is at least very, very missing. Information leading to the safe return of Ronan Boyle to the Special Unit headquarters in Killarney will be rewarded. No questions asked.

An ever-so-polite reminder that reprinting this manuscript in whole or in part, or even quoting it in an offhanded, "just me and my mates having a goof" sort of way, will be prosecuted to the fullest extent of human and faerie law.

Some of Boyle's original notes appear to have been scribbled in the dark and are reprinted here as close as anyone could guess. Evidence on the papers is confusing, as the garda laboratory in Dublin has confirmed that the ink is both human blood—some Boyle's and some not Boyle's—as well as the blood of two different male leprechauns, plus one kind of fudge.

In short: The statements in the following text represent the views and opinions exclusively of Ronan Boyle (posthumous?), Lieutenant, Garda Special Unit of Tir Na Nog. They do not reflect the views or opinions of the An Garda Síochána itself or the government of the Republic of Ireland.

With my best wishes and hoping not to prosecute you to the fullest extent of the law,

F.D., D.C.

TIR·NA·NOG

SHENANOGRAM

Chapter One

THE NARROWEST FELLOW

6 December

It almost never snows in Ireland. Ireland is a temperate zone. Snow-wise, the best you can hope for is a dusting. If most Irish snows were Parmesan cheese on your spaghetti, you would gesture to the waiter and say, "More, *per favore*—that isn't nearly enough."

But Tuesday the sixth of December was a bona fide blizzard.

When my phone buzzed at four thirty in the morning,

I was in a profound coma. The night before had been the retirement party of Captain John Fearnley. Fearnley is a lovely man who had been like a father figure to me since the scandal. Two years ago, I was sitting on a metal file cabinet in his office, as there are no extra chairs. Fearnley prefers that no one talk to him for a length of time that would necessitate them sitting down, but he made an exception for me on my first day.

"Gonna make a basket. Awesome?" he said, handing me half of his tuna sandwich, his eyes filled with kindness.

He may in fact have said: "Gonna make the best of it, aren't you, son?" but I couldn't be sure. Fearnley has the kind of country accent that is almost impossible to understand, even for Irish people. I took the sandwich and had a bite. I'd never eaten a tuna sandwich before, and the smell was intriguing.

"Thank you, sir," I said as my face went flush and tears welled up in my eyes.

"Sauron. Lettuce. Tall stout," he mumbled, tousling my hair and very likely saying: "It's all right, son. Let it all out."

But I wasn't crying, despite my sorry state. Tuna had just been added to the list of things to which I am very allergic. If you have food allergies like me, you'll know the best thing to do in this circumstance is to make yourself throw up, which I did. There was a brief pause. Fearnley didn't make a fuss, and he didn't judge. The kindness never left his eyes.

"Idris Elba, Idris Elba," said Fearnley, handing me his handkerchief.

I am fairly certain that this was actually "Clean yerself up, clean yerself up."

Then he gave me two euros for the Fanta machine, because he's the type of everyday hero who does things like this.

Now, two years later, it was four thirty in the morning, and my mobile phone was *vrrrrrrrrrrrring*. The view out the window of my shared flat looks directly onto Galway Bay. The sun wouldn't be up for almost four more hours.

Between the waves crashing on the seawall and the snow driving sideways, Galway did not look like a planet I would want to visit without a space suit.

I had been asleep for approximately three hours. I looked to the mirror, expecting to present a sad state, but was pleasantly surprised to see I looked so very handsome. This was because I was not yet wearing my glasses. I put them on and saw that I was still, in fact, regular Ronan Boyle, the nearsighted, gangly person that I was the night before, but somehow even worse, as I'd only slept for approximately three hours.

The voice on the opposite end of my phone kicked me out of my slumber. It was a mysterious garda* officer named Pat Finch, whose ghoulish face is so crisscrossed with bright red veins that it looks like a map of hell drawn by a monk in a medieval lunatic asylum. Pat Finch looks like what a heart attack would look like if it could walk around eating fish-and-chips and saying terrible things about

---

* The Irish word for *police*.

Roscommon Football Club's starting lineup. But underneath all of that on the outside—Pat Finch is really just a nasty person.

Pat Finch was not someone you wanted on the other end of your phone at any time of day. But here he was. Or rather in my brain, it seemed, because he was yelling so very loudly.

"Is this Boyle with the Galway garda?" he bellowed.

"Aye," I replied. "But there are two Boyles in the Galway office, sir. I suspect you must want the other one—Conor, he's the ranking sergeant. I'm the younger one—Ronan, intern in the evidence department."

"Are you the little skinny one?" he asked.

I wasn't sure how to respond to this. By all accounts, I am fairly thin. Not from a strict regimen, but as a byproduct of many severe allergies and being a terrible cook.

"Yes, I suppose," I said.

"THEN GET YOUR SKINNY BEHIND OUT HERE

TO CLIFDEN, YOU EEJIT," and with a wet snort that sounded like a boar with a mouthful of macaroni, he hung up.

Clifden? I thought to myself, as I was the only person there to think anything. Dolores, my flatmate, was nowhere to be seen. (Dolores is my legal guardian and has been ever since the scandal two years ago. She is a professional busker in Galway and one of the most beautiful fiddle players you'll ever meet. She is also very popular, which means I'm almost always on my own, without a legal guardian. This is fine by me, as Dolores is an absolute delight, but not great with domestic things and positively terrible with kids.)

There was a bit of trouble getting myself immediately to Clifden, because I can't drive, I have no car, and I did not know what Clifden was. It's not a town, as I had thought. Clifden is a castle out on the coast in Connemara. It was almost two hours before I got there via the 923 Coach.* By then the blizzard had dissipated into rain, as Ireland is a temperate zone, and it hardly ever snows.

---

* Bus.

Later, I would mark this trip to Clifden Castle as the day that changed my life forever. The events of the next few hours were so confusing that I managed to forget that today, the sixth of December, was also my fifteenth birthday.

When I arrived, there were several garda vehicles on site and a sleek military jeep that I almost couldn't see, except for its tires. The body was covered in a green camouflage that blended perfectly with the field beyond it. The jeep's license plate was a bit spooky—black and gold, bearing just the image of a harp and the number seven. *Who the devil gets that sort of license plate with almost no numbers at all?* I wondered to myself, as wondering things to myself is eighty-five percent of what I do.

I should point out that Clifden Castle is actually just the ruins of a castle and has been for at least ninety years. But saying "Clifden Castle ruins" takes too long, so no one does that.

As I jogged through the mush toward the ruins, Pat Finch climbed out of the jeep and rushed up toward me. His version of the garda uniform was unfamiliar to me.

His face made me gasp, as it's straight out of a Kabuki nightmare.

"Are you Boyle?" he shouted.

I nodded.

"You're just a boy? Ha. Brilliant. Follow me," he said with an evil glint in his eye. "Meet the captain, and stick these in your nose if you know what's good for you."

Finch handed me a pair of regular orange plugs, and I stuck them in my nostrils as I had been instructed. This says a lot about human nature, for if some street kook in Eyre Square had told me to shove orange plugs into my nose, I would have told him to get stuffed. But Pat Finch is an imposing figure.

We wound our way through the ruins, and Finch clicked on his torch,* leading me down a moldy spiral of stone steps into the depths of the castle. We descended into a set of caverns that must have served as storage rooms when the castle was still functioning. It was cold down there, but at

---

* The Irish word for *flashlight*.

least it wasn't raining. Steam was puffing only out of our mouths, as our noses were safely and orangely plugged. For no reason at all, I said to Pat Finch, "Perfect place to store cheese, eh?" Because I say very stupid things when I'm nervous, and right then an impending sense of dread was filling my stomach.

We entered a cavern, and I followed Pat Finch toward some work lights that had been arranged around a strange little crime scene. Several Connemara Garda officers were hustling about, searching with torches, as were officers wearing the same curious uniform as Pat Finch, each carrying a wooden shillelagh,* which seemed odd to me at the time.

---

* One of these:

In a moment, I would understand why our noses were plugged: because leprechauns, especially when they're trapped or in distress, can create awful smells. It's a defense mechanism, much like that of a skunk, to which leprechauns are not at all related.

And I was about to meet my first leprechaun.

When I saw the little man, I gasped so hard that I popped the earplugs from my nose. My nostrils were instantly flooded with the smell of the worst fish soup in the history of the world. Soup that if served to them would make French prisoners riot. I scrambled to replug my nose. Pat Finch hiked his straining belt and said, "He's musking. It's how you know the little devil is lying." He gave the leprechaun a firm kick. The leprechaun hissed back at him.

As I had never seen a real live leprechaun before, I then did what any sensible person would do and let out a high-pitched scream that sounded like a teenage parrot passing through a wood chipper.

I thought I must have been dreaming, back in my bed in Galway. I kicked myself in the shin with my heel to check

if I was awake, and the pain was both a brief distraction from the chill in my bones and solid confirmation that I was awake.

Pat Finch then gave a kick to my *other* shin.

"Ouch!" I screamed.

"Just giving you a second opinion," said Pat Finch. "You're not dreaming. Now keep your eyes open and your mouth shut. And if he tries to give you gold, don't take it. Never take gold from one of these devils."

I nodded, wincing at the now perfectly balanced pain.

The leprechaun in custody was a male, approximately twenty-eight inches tall. (At this time, I did not know that leprechauns are more powerful the smaller that they are. While I have not met him in person, I have been told by those who have that Raghnall, King of Tir Na Nog, is less than eleven inches tall and probably the ugliest thing that has ever lived.)

This leprechaun was a relatively weak adult male. His name we did not know yet, as it is a rule with faerie folk that you have to guess their names, which is very time-consuming.*

This leprechaun's face looked like a potato that had somehow had a baby with another potato, and then that potato baby grew to be a thousand years old and got very constipated. His beet-red beard was tinged with ashes, and his eyes were fixed in a permanent squint from the centuries of pipe smoke† that had wafted up at them.

The commanding officer on the scene was Captain Siobhán de Valera, who is a distant descendant of Eamon de

---

* Later, when I came to work in the office of the Garda Special Unit of Tir Na Nog, I would create an app for faerie name-guessing, and it's been a real time-saver.

† All leprechauns, male and female, smoke clay pipes, which is disgusting. It's also why leaving a clay pipe by your fireplace is such an easy way to catch a leprechaun. This is something humans used to do until they realized that leprechauns *do not mean well at all*. In my many years in the Garda of Tir Na Nog, I have come across precisely two cases where a human caught a leprechaun and actually received a crock of gold, no strings attached. Leprechauns are unrivaled in their devilish cleverness and will go to great lengths to trick and befuddle humans. They also bite, can create foul smells, and will whack you with a shillelagh so hard on your kneecap that it will shatter. Knee replacement surgery is covered by insurance for Garda of Tir Na Nog officers as it is such a common occurrence.

Valera, once the president of Ireland. The captain is a serious, handsome woman with jet-black hair that she keeps in a tight bun. She was wearing high boots with leather knee-cap protectors, and in her gloved hand she twirled one of the finest fighting shillelaghs I've ever seen.* It was made from oak root—almost purple in color and as hard as a lead pipe. The air made a pleasant whirring sound as she twirled her shillelagh. The captain paced with a scowl on her face that I would later find out was a permanent fixture.

"Domhnall the Intrepid? Brian the Bold?" she whispered at the leprechaun. She was trying to guess his name, as by possessing a leprechaun's name you can wield tremendous psychological advantage over them.

"Don't bother with that. He's been read his Republic Rights. Just have him tell Boyle here where the changeling is," grunted Pat Finch. Republic Rights are the rights that faerie folk have when they are outside of Tir Na Nog and in the human Republic of Ireland.

---

* Shillelaghs are mostly for fighting, it turns out; they just pose as walking sticks when not being used for fighting.

Captain de Valera turned in my direction, and her mismatched eyes shot right through me. Siobhán de Valera has one green eye and one brown eye, which takes a bit of getting used to. Her uniform was different from that of ordinary garda officers. On her long leather coat was a badge with the Irish word CAPTAEN on it, and you can probably guess what that means. Across her back was a strap with quick-release, gold carabiner hooks, which is how all Tir Na Nog Garda carry their fighting shillelaghs. On her belt was a befuddling array of accessories: a small electric torch, a bandolier of clay pipes—just the right size for leprechauns—a standard-issue garda electric Taser, two flares, a flask of Jameson whiskey, and then two other tiny flasks labeled with Irish words I didn't know at the time.

In truth, what I did not know at the time could fill a book, which is what I am attempting to remedy here in this diary. Like all Irish children, I had heard of the wee folk—leprechauns, far darrigs, harpies, and such—and that they love mischief and they come from Tir Na Nog, which is the land of the faerie folk. But like most sensible children, I always assumed that this was a bunch of made-up blarney— stories invented and embellished in pubs by glassy-eyed old-timers who were pissed as farts on rum and punch.

But let me assure you of the fact that I was about to learn, on this day, the day that I did not recall was my fifteenth birthday:

Tir Na Nog is a real place.

And the wee folk are not a friendly pack of elves who will fill your shoes with candy while you sleep. They are small, hard-drinking swindlers who would steal your nose and replace it with a turnip if they thought they could make one single euro from doing it. There are also more types of wee folk than I had ever imagined, and if you knew how frequently and freely they travel into the human Republic of Ireland, passing right under your bed, you would have trouble sleeping. Some of the faerie folk are delightful. Some are disgusting. As for my involvement with the Garda Special Unit of Tir Na Nog, I will relate to you the events of my education as they unfolded—unless the details are of a case still being investigated by the Special Unit headquarters in Killarney.

Captain de Valera paced. On her belt, I could see more oddities—a pouch of tobacco and tiny handcuffs with an old Celtic symbol. Leprechauns cannot be held in handcuffs unless you can also distract them with a clever poem that highlights their peril and plays into their inherent narcissism. This detail keeps a lot of qualified candidates out of the Garda of Tir Na Nog, as instantaneous poem writing while in a crisis situation can be a trick.

Captain Siobhán de Valera stepped toward me, sizing me up. She raised her purple shillelagh. I flinched backward, until I realized she was doing it to measure me and not to whack me. She checked the distance across my shoulders and then my hips as if she were planning to make me a suit, or perhaps a coffin.

"Well done, Finch," said the captain. "He's practically a pole. He'll do nicely if my theory is right."

"Ronan Boyle. He was the narrowest garda in our records," shrugged Pat Finch. "An intern—all the way from Galway."

If no one's ever said this about you, let me tell you that it is distressing indeed. The knot in my stomach started to somersault on itself as I imagined being used as some sort of pole, here in the depths of the ruins of Clifden Castle several hundred feet belowground and way out in Connemara, where nobody knows me. Who would even notify Dolores, my guardian and one of the most beautiful fiddle players you've ever seen?

"This leprechaun has replaced a human baby with a changeling," Pat Finch belched to me as he gave the leprechaun another swift kick. "And Captain de Valera thinks you may be just the lad for the job."

"He's stolen the baby from the Republic and replaced it

with this," said Captain de Valera as she held up a particularly ugly log. The log was dressed in baby clothes with a terrifying face carved into its upper portion. On a small branch that protruded where a child's arm might be, there was an evidence tag marking it as EXHIBIT A.

The leprechaun giggled in a fit of glee as the captain held up the log, delighted with his handiwork, sending toots of pipe smoke out of his little snout like a devilish steam engine. His pockets jangled with what was clearly a lot of gold.

Captain de Valera twirled her shillelagh pensively. "When I saw this log, carved with such meticulous craftsmanship into a changeling for a human baby, I knew it must be the work of one of the great leprechaun carvers of Tir Na Nog," she said as she paced the cavern. The steam from her nostrils made me aware for the first time that she was not wearing nose plugs. She was used to the foul smell of leprechauns when they are musking.

"There's no way this changeling was carved by any

other than Tagdh of the Floating Lakes," the captain pronounced, and she tossed the log to a junior garda officer on the perimeter of the crime scene. "Pack it up and label it: changeling log, carved by Tagdh, greatest of the leprechaun tricksters, not this amateur we've captured here. Why, this wee fellow here would probably make a changeling out of peat. Pack it up, lads, we're done."

There was a strange glow in the cavern. I turned to see that the leprechaun's face was now steaming red, with vapor rising from it as he twitched like a steel teakettle left in a microwave by someone who has never read the instructions for a microwave.

Captain de Valera turned and gave me the smallest smile you could imagine. A moment later, the leprechaun bolted up, spilling gold coins everywhere as he howled: "TAGDH OF THE FLOATING LAKES NEVER CARVED A CHANGELING LOG THAT WELL IN HIS WILDEST DREAMS! 'TWAS CARVED BY ME OWN SELF! I, RAURI, KILLER OF UNICORNS!"

And with that, Captain de Valera spun, knocking the leprechaun's hat off with her shillelagh. She extended her hand to meet his tiny one. "Ah. Rauri, Killer of Unicorns. Pleased to make your acquaintance," she whispered in his ear with a devilish smile.

The leprechaun, now name-known and registered as Rauri, Killer of Unicorns, fumed. He'd just been tricked into telling us his name and had his hat knocked off—which turns out to be a major insult to faerie folk.

A garda officer with a camera popped in and snapped off a few pictures of Rauri, front and profile. Another officer measured his height and his beard with a bronze staff, and a third knelt down and did a charcoal rubbing of the underside of his little shoe. This was before I knew that leprechaun shoes are the best-made things in either our world or Tir Na Nog. Leprechauns will spend centuries perfecting their shoes. The buckles are made from solid gold. According to tradition, leprechaun kings and queens never dance—even at a wedding or céilí.*

---

* *Céilí* means dance, celebration, or party.

Some thought this was because it was undignified for faerie royals, but the reality is that their shoes are simply far too heavy, with gold and jewel-encrusted buckles that outweigh their entire body. As for the charcoal rubbing the officer was making—this is standard policy when registering a new leprechaun in the files of the Garda of Tir Na Nog, as the soles of leprechaun shoes are as distinct as snowflakes, no two being alike.

Rauri, Killer of Unicorns, fumed and kicked. He then did something that leprechauns only do when they are very angry—he snapped his pipe in half. A few of the garda officers gasped at the sight of it.

"File that shoe print in Killarney, and while you're at it, run a check to see if any unicorns are missing in Tir Na Nog," said Pat Finch to the officer with the charcoal sketch as Rauri fidgeted, alternately fuming with rage and then weeping over his broken pipe.

I didn't know it then, but the likelihood that this Rauri was actually a "killer of unicorns" was precisely zero. The average unicorn stands fifteen hands high* from its hooves to its withers, and the horn on its head is not for show. Yes, unicorn horns can make dirty water clean, but the horn's real purpose is as a weapon—very specifically, for killing leprechauns. The horns, or "dowsers" as the unicorns call them, are as hard and sharp as diamonds and could poke through an armored tank as if it were a soggy cheese sandwich that you had forgotten about after a long, wonderful day trip to the beach.

Leprechauns love boastful names like Rauri, Killer of Unicorns. The more pretentious the name, the better. Later on, I would meet and befriend "Owen, Handsomest Fellow of the Sugar Marshes Ever," and "Aileen, Whose Luscious Eyes Sparkle Like Ten Thousand Emeralds in the Sun." (He wasn't, and they don't.) Yet both of these are totally normal leprechaun names. It would be as if your name was "Sheila, Who Is Better Than Adele at Singing." Leprechauns are confused by the mundanity

---

* A hand is four inches.

of our human names and see them as a sign of our low self-esteem.

Captain de Valera let her fingers casually flick one of the clay pipes on her belt. Rauri's eyes seized upon it like a starving man as they began to well up with tears.

"Care for a new pipe, would you?" she asked him, knowing full well the answer was a million times yes.

"Aye, miss. Let Rauri, Killer of Unicorns, have one of yours! You've so many to spare!" he pleaded in his leprechaun accent, which sounds a lot like a human from Dingle who's had a strong dose of helium.

"Tell nice Mr. Boyle from Galway here where the human baby is, and we'll see about that pipe," said the captain.

Rauri's eyes darted back and forth. He was clearly torn about revealing the location of the baby, but the notion of a new clay pipe was just too much to resist.

"I was within my rights to change that baby!" Rauri cried out. "The parents of that ugly, stupid baby caught me at the end of the faintest rainbow you ever saw in your entire life. I told 'em I would give 'em no gold, but that if they let me go, I would talk to the horses at Ballinrobe Raceway and find out which one was going to win the derby the next day—making them as rich as twenty sultans."

Captain de Valera smacked the back of my head with her shillelagh. "Why aren't you writing this down, Boyle?"

I fumbled to extract my notebook from my trousers and began to copy down the leprechaun's story. This was technically my first official act in the Garda Special Unit of Tir Na Nog, the division of the Irish National Police that oversees crimes of the faerie folk.

"I was as good as my word," said Rauri. "The fools set me free, and I made haste to the racetrack at Ballinrobe, stopping only for a wee bit of the juice of the barley with my mate Mike, who is a troll under a bridge on the Robe River."

"Which bridge?" asked Siobhán de Valera.

"The stone one with the fork at Creagh Road," whimpered Rauri, his eyes locked on the pipe, which Siobhán was now casually spinning in her fingers. "Go and ask Mike. He'll tell you for sure that I was on my way to Ballinrobe, and I did as I said."

Pat Finch nodded to a garda officer. "Send a car around to Creagh Road and see if this Mike the Troll will back up the little man's story here," he said. The officer nodded and departed.*

"So Mike the Troll and I made merry under his bridge, and then he decided to join me, and we made off to the racetrack," said Rauri. "When we arrived at the paddock at Ballinrobe, the horses were still awake, nervous about the race the next afternoon. Mike and I thought that the least we could do was be sociable and share some of our strong whiskey with these poor, dim-witted horses. Which we

---

* All bridges in Ireland have trolls that live under them, which on the surface sounds horrifying, as bridge trolls eat goats and children without manners. But since 1963, bridge trolls have been protected by Irish law and the World Wildlife Fund, because they had been hunted nearly into extinction. In exchange for this protection, Sharon, Queen of the Trolls, made an accord with the Irish government that bridge trolls would eat only very sickly goats and truly horrible children. And for the most part they have held up their part of this accord, which many people say accounts for Ireland's population of hearty goats and respectful boys and girls.

did, and I'd be lying if I didn't tell you that the whiskey and craic* flowed until a wee hour."

At this point my hand was practically frozen stiff as I wrote down the leprechaun's story. I dropped my pen, which skittered across the stone floor. I blew on my fingers to warm them up, but even my breath was cold down there in the caverns, so that didn't do much good. Captain de Valera shot me an annoyed look, although it may have just been a regular look, and her mismatched eyes and permascowl made it seem like I was a target for her shillelagh again.

"Sorry," I blurted. "Just trying to keep up," I said, collecting my pen from the ground.

Pat Finch snorted and tugged at his belt, which seemed to be in endless escape mission from his tummy toward the ground. The captain took a small pouch of tobacco off of her belt and began to methodically pack the clay pipe. Rauri's lips trembled as he reached for the pipe, and she gently pressed back against his hands with her shillelagh.

---

* Fun and gossip.

"Get to the point," said Captain de Valera. "Where is the baby?"

"Mike and I got a wee bit drunk with the horses, who gave us the inside scoop—that the one among them called Hold Me Closer Tiny Dancer would be the winning horse at the derby," said Rauri the leprechaun. "We thanked the horses and left. And if Mike ate one of the smaller horses named Bingo Was His Name-O, well, I can't recall if that happened at all, and I'm not even sure why I would mention it."

"Shall I ring the racetrack and see if a horse has been eaten?" I asked in an unplanned effort to seem useful.

"Indeed, Mr. Boyle," said Captain de Valera. "And radio the lads on their way to question Mike the Troll and tell 'em to check the bridge for horse bones. Eating a draught horse is a fifty-euro fine, but eating a racehorse could mean a year in the Joy Vaults," said the captain pointedly to Rauri as she poked his chest with the tip of her shillelagh.

The Joy Vaults is a slang term for the subterranean cells beneath the Mountjoy Prison in Dublin, sometimes called "the Joy."

The aboveground levels of Mountjoy Prison hold Ireland's medium-security human prisoners. It's a place with which I am familiar, as I have spent the third Tuesday of each month there in the badly lit visitors' ward. After the scandal, my parents, Brendan and Fiona Boyle, became inmates, numbers 477738 and 477739. More on that in a moment.

The Joy Vaults are the nine subterranean levels of the prison, lake, and stables that are reserved for the faerie folk, sheeries, banshees, leprechauns, unicorns, etc., who violate the laws of the Republic of Ireland. The first three levels down are minimum security, and the bottom six are reserved for more serious offenders. After years in the garda, I have still only seen the first four levels. The ninth level I'm told is strictly for banshees, whose appearance always harbingers the death of a human. As a result, the lower levels of the Joy Vaults are not guarded by human officers but by deputized leprechauns.

"I returned Mike under his bridge and made it back to the parents of that ugly, ugly, unkind baby," said Rauri.

"I told them about Hold Me Closer Tiny Dancer, and they went to Ballinrobe that day, and they bet their life savings on the mare."

"And she lost!" I shouted out like a person who has watched a lot of Sherlock Holmes on the telly, which I am. "Because she was so drunk on your leprechaun whiskey!"

"No, you eejit," replied Rauri. "She won. All of the horses were drunk, and one of them may or may not have been eaten by Mike the Troll. The parents of that hideous, sarcastic baby were exactly as I had promised—as rich as twenty sultans. I thought it was only fair that I get a wee finder's fee for all me troubles. They disagreed and set about to kill me with a hurley stick. I lay in wait in a nearby well, and then, by cover of night, I returned and swapped their baby for this magnificently carved log. ONE HUNDRED PERCENT WITHIN MY RIGHTS. LOOK IT UP!"

The air hung heavy for a moment. Captain de Valera shot Pat Finch a look. "He's not wrong," she said. "Write up the baby's parents for Second-Degree Tinkering with Faerie Folk, and Rauri here will get a one-hundred-euro fine for making a changeling."

"Aye, ma'am," said Pat Finch.

"Now, is the baby hidden where I suspect it is?" asked the captain of the wee man.

"Aye. Down the oubliette," whimpered Rauri. And with that, the captain handed him the new clay pipe, loaded with fresh tobacco. Rauri struck a match on his nose and lit the pipe, sucking in a huge plume of smoke as if he'd been underwater and the tobacco was fresh air. He giggled with glee as Captain de Valera turned to me, her permanent scowl remaining precisely as it always looked.

"The oubliette. This is what I had feared. And that's where you come in, Ronan Boyle," she said.

"I will do my best, ma'am," I replied, my voice sounding weaker than I had expected. Perhaps because I had now had the nose plugs in for so long, combined with the frigid cavern air and approximately three hours of sleep.

"You're just the lad," said the captain as her eyes fixed

on a narrow hole in the wall of the cavern. "Do you know what an oubliette is?"

"No, ma'am," I replied.

And it was true. At this point I had no idea what one was, but was only moments away from never forgetting.

"'Oubliette' is from the French for 'to forget,'" she said as two garda officers started to forcefully attach mountain climbing straps to my midsection. "In some old castles, it was a shaft where they would dump the bodies of their enemies. The bottom was sometimes lined with spikes. And down there their foes would be quite literally forgotten," said the captain.

"Like a fast-acting dungeon," chuckled Pat Finch, the veins in his face pulsing like a jack-o'-lantern whose candle was about to flicker out from a strong cross-breeze.

The two garda officers attached a clamp to the harness on my back and began unfurling a hundred feet of nylon rope, which they secured around my middle.

"This oubliette was sealed up," said the captain. "Without a wrecking ball, the opening will only fit the narrowest possible fellow."

I understood now that I had been called into this case simply because I, Ronan Boyle, was the narrowest possible fellow. The only one who would fit into the hole.

And now it was my job to be lowered into the oubliette and collect the human baby that Rauri, Killer of Unicorns, had stashed down there. I pulled out my nose plugs to get a few deep breaths. The musking, fish soup smell had changed and was now a tobacco and fish soup smell, which was somehow even more atrocious.

I stepped toward the hole. Making myself as narrow as I could, I pulled myself into it. A profound darkness wrapped me up like a blanket. Captain de Valera passed her torch in after me. I fumbled for it and clicked it on. The officers on the other end of the rope started to lower me down.

Chapter Two

THE OUBLIETTE

s I descended into the oubliette, it felt as if I had three hearts: one in my chest and two others pounding in my eardrums. The electric torch only illuminated the stone wall three inches in front of my face, and I decided it would be better just to close my eyes until the rope had lowered me down far enough to feel the floor or the crunchy bones or whatever horror show awaited me at the bottom of this dreadful abyss.

A moment later, to my surprise, I was comfortably in

my favorite movie theater, watching *My Life as a Dog* and eating a smoked Gouda and marmite sandwich with Dame Judi Dench.

In reality, I wasn't actually in a movie theater with Dame Judi Dench, but if you're like me, when you start to have a panic attack, you go to a happy place inside your imagination. And this is mine: my favorite movie theater, with my favorite actress, watching my favorite film. And in my imagination, Dame Judi leans over to me and says, "Ronan Boyle, this is the best sandwich I've ever had in my entire life." And I reply, "Please shut up, Dame Judi Dench," as it's rude to talk even in an imaginary movie theater, and she of all people should know this.

A moment later, I was yanked out of my happy place and back to reality by the soft thump of my feet on the floor of the oubliette. I shined the torch around to get my bearings, but soon realized I didn't need it, as the room was somehow supplying its own illumination.

There were remnants of ancient bones and a few

human skulls scattered about. I chose not to make direct eye contact with any of their empty eye sockets in an effort to bolster my courage. I followed the golden glow, looking for the source, kicking aside some old barrels and rubbish that had piled up over the ages, trying not to think of what, or rather who, was making the sound of crunching bones under my feet.

"Are you all the way down?" called the captain from the shaft above me.

"I think I am!" I yelled up stupidly, as I tend to say very stupid things when I'm nervous. "There's something glowing down here. Maybe a small fire or lamp?"

As I got closer to the light, I began to hear the most gorgeous harp music my ears have ever known. I reached the corner of the room, and there amongst some old crates was the baby itself, wrapped up safe and sound and fast asleep. (And yes, Rauri was not wrong—it was a fairly ugly baby, by both human and leprechaun standards.)

Little did I know that I, too, would be fast asleep in a

few moments, because the glow and music were coming from a jinx harp.*

I had just picked up both the baby and the harp and stuffed them into my jacket, buttoning them up snugly for safekeeping, when I felt the overwhelming urge to take a good, hard nap. I gently laid back and cracked the back of my skull on the stone floor. I felt the warm trickle of blood beneath my hair and drifted off into a deep, jinx-harp-induced sleep.

Twenty minutes later, wearing just my underwear and jacket, my legs covered in fresh scrapes, I was awakened by the ghoulish face of Pat Finch, who was now wearing large protective headphones, like an airport worker.

"Jinx harp got ya, kid," he laughed, as if my state was anything to laugh about.

---

* A jinx harp is probably the most pleasant weapon in all of Tir Na Nog. It's not very complicated—just a regular harp that's been buried with someone who died under mysterious circumstances, then dug up again on a full moon and baptized by a sheerie in one of the Floating Lakes. The harp, then bewitched, will sing, and its song will induce sleep in anyone who hears it. It's a favorite weapon of the wee folk—perhaps because it's nonlethal and subsequently not subject to fines from the Garda of Tir Na Nog.

"The baby's fine. And we sealed up the harp in a sound-proof case," said the captain, taking off her headphones. "But I'm afraid it was quite a struggle to pull you out of there in your unconscious state. Your trousers must have caught on something on the way up, and we lost them."

"Either you can go back down for them, as you're the only one who fits in the hole, or we can get you a spare rain slicker," added Pat Finch.

I checked with the captain's torch down the shaft and could just barely make out the silhouette of my trousers some ten meters below, hooked on the edge of a cornerstone, ripped and fluttering like the saddest flag of surrender. I decided it was not worth a second trip into the shaft and accepted the rain slicker that an officer handed to me. I tied it around my waist like a makeshift kilt. I pity those who had to see me in this state: glasses fogged up, plastic kilt, and scraped knees—everyone averted their eyes, except for Captain de Valera. She stepped toward me and put a gentle hand to rest on my shoulder, gazing at me with her mismatched eyes, and said sincerely: "Pull your miserable self together, Boyle, before I knock the daylights out of you. You've just been transferred. I want you to come work for me."

My pride and my knees were injured, but it seems I had passed some test of bravery that qualified me to start as a trainee in the Garda Special Unit of Tir Na Nog, one of the most ancient and enigmatic law enforcement agencies in Europe.

Looking back on it, descending into a cave of bones to find a very ugly baby would be one of the easiest days that I would have in that first year under Captain Siobhán de Valera's command.

After that, things got complicated.

CHAPTER THREE

THE SCANDAL

I returned to my shared flat in Galway that afternoon with orders to report to the offices of the Garda Special Unit in Killarney for the twelve-week training program. I was told to be there by nine P.M. sharp on Thursday—two days hence. Nine P.M. is the start of the normal workday for the Tir Na Nog Unit, as so much of the mischief of faerie folk happens after dark, and many of the suspects are nocturnal creatures by nature, such as clurichauns, who are slightly taller than leprechauns but much nastier, and the far darrig, who are disgusting-looking little red creatures with snouts and tails who are actually lovely in person.

Dolores, my beautiful flatmate, was home for the first time in ages. She gave me a bear hug, spilling some of her industrial-sized margarita down my back, because that is her style. Dolores lives in the moment, and she's never going to deny herself a margarita in the afternoon, no matter what you or anybody else says about it. She's a delight, and probably the most unreliable legal guardian a boy could have.

"I'd hate to see what the other guy's pants look like," she said in reference to my impromptu kilt, because Dolores always says hilarious things, and she knows exactly how to cheer me up.

Dolores is not a blood relative of mine, which makes her an unusual choice for a court-appointed guardian. Dolores was a student getting university credit to help my parents at the National Museum at the time of the scandal.

The scandal must be addressed sooner or later, so let's do it right now and get that part over with, as it's not the finest hour of the Boyle family. To this day, I maintain that my parents are innocent, and one day I will prove it.

My parents are lovely people who got caught up in a nefarious crime ring. If you haven't heard of the Bog Man Scandal, it caused quite a bit of legal rawmaish* at the time, and it's also the reason that my security clearance in the Special Unit will never be top level, as I have "known associates" who are convicted criminals: Mum and Da.

My parents were not lifelong criminals. Quite the opposite. They were quiet, bookish types—curators at the National Museum of Ireland, Merrion Street Upper, Dublin 2, Ireland.

Curator is a fancy word that means they were responsible for looking after artifacts, arranging the galleries, cataloging, and so forth. They also spent a great deal of time out in the field, collecting archaeological pieces—which, it turns out, can be very-very-super-illegal.†

---

* Hubbub.

† It's against the law even to use a metal detector in Ireland. No joke, look it up. Of course, you don't have to look it up, because I just told you.

Treasure hunting in Ireland is only forbidden if the artifacts are not handed over immediately to the National Museum, which Mum and Da seemed to have "forgotten" to do at one point. Mum and Da always had a disproportionate number of metal detectors around the house, which in hindsight does throw up a bit of a red flag.

According to the charges in *Republic v. Boyle*, my parents had amassed a treasure trove of Iron and Bronze Age objects that they sold to a shady art dealer named Lord Desmond Dooley on Henrietta Street in Dublin. (*Lord* is not a title; that's his actual first name. Yes, creepy. Who does that? What must his parents have been like?)

Lord Desmond Dooley is an icky man of about five feet tall, with the pinched-up face of a gargoyle who just caught a whiff of cat barf.

Dooley was the ringleader of this stolen treasures operation, yet it was his testimony that secured my parents' conviction. Dooley wept on the stand and accepted a plea bargain. He remains a free man to this very day.

If you believe Dooley, *which you should not*, my parents sold artifacts to his underground gallery in Dublin. He in turn dealt them to international collectors at staggering prices. The loot included ancient bronze jewelry, Viking helmets, and weapons.*

The thefts of the Viking items and jewelry were considered misdemeanors, but there was one stolen treasure in particular for which no sensible person would forgive my parents: the Bog Man.

The Bog Man is a mummy. Yes. No kidding. My parents unearthed him on one of their treasure hunts in Offaly. Mummies are not uncommon in Ireland, as the ground is made of peat, which is a remarkable preservative. Sometimes you will find very old humans who fell into the peat and nobody noticed for a bit, until they popped up hundreds of years later, having missed all of their appointments. Thanks to the bogs, there may, in fact, be more mummies in Ireland than in Egypt, only people try to find

---

* The Vikings had two bases in Ireland from which to go around whacking cheerful, unsuspecting Irish people on the head.

the Irish ones less often, since they weren't buried with chariots and solid-gold patio furniture.

There are a few bog mummies on display in the National Museum. They tend to look like eyeball-less people who have been dehydrated into shiny beef jerky. But this particular Bog Man was special—as testing revealed that he had been preserved for over four thousand years.

This would make him Ireland's oldest known thing.

Lord Desmond Dooley claims that my parents offered to sell him the Bog Man and a few other treasures. He met them at their home laboratory in the wee hours of the night. According to his version: My parents got cold feet and fled with the Bog Man and Dooley's money.

Mum and Da's version of events is that Dooley stole the Bog Man from their lab before they could hand it over to the museum. That's why Dooley came in the wee hours of the night—and he wasn't alone. He and his accomplices took the Bog Man, planted the money on Mum and Da, and then reported Mum and Da to the police as they fled.

Lord Desmond Dooley is a wealthy and unscrupulous

man with powerful friends in the courts. And many people mistakenly think he is some kind of lord, even though that is just his first name—the same way that the singer Lorde's first name is Ella.

The Bog Man hasn't been found since that night, but I am certain that Dooley either sold it or has it in his possession, hidden away until it's safe to sell.

Two years ago, on the night of my parents' arrest, the three of us were lying on the kitchen floor playing "Are You There, Moriarty?" This is a fun parlor game where you are blindfolded on the ground, and you try to whack the other players with a rolled-up newspaper. Players are only allowed to ask, "Are you there, Moriarty?" And the other player must respond, "Yes." Then the newspaper whacking may commence. Technically, the first person to get bonked loses, but in the excitement of the game, many whacks are often landed before a winner is declared. It's an uncomplicated affair and just about the most fun you can have.

My folks, Brendan and Fiona Boyle, are experts in Irish history and also at this game.

"Are you there, Moriarty?" my mum had just asked me, trying to bounce her voice around the room like radar.

"Yes," I responded, as those are the rules and that's the only thing you can say. I was tucked against the far wall. There was no way she could bonk me, even with the extra-long newspaper roll she was using. Fiona Boyle took a fierce swing that sounded like a direct hit against the stove.

"Ow!"

"Ha!" said Da. "Go, lad, go! You'll never catch him! He's a proper Boyle, quick as Mercury, like his old man!"

This was an exaggeration. No Boyles are athletes of any kind. I once saw my da reading and humming along to Taylor Swift's "Bad Blood" at the same time, and this level of exertion caused him to panic and spill soup all over the cat.

I spun across the linoleum, taking several swats at where I expected Mum to be, but Fiona Boyle is even narrower than I am, and she can roll like a dry noodle.

"Freeze!" said a voice.

"Not fair!" I yelled. "You can't say that, it's not allowed."

"Freeze and put yer hands where I can see 'em," continued the voice.

Now it was clear that this voice was neither Mum nor Da. Turns out this voice was Monty Heneghan of the Dublin Garda, a deadly serious detective with the face of a baby that requires burping.

Detective Heneghan bursting into our house while we were all blindfolded on the kitchen floor made his arrival extra surprising. We pulled off our blindfolds to see that there were, in fact, two officers standing in the kitchen: Detective Heneghan and another man who looked like a meerkat. How long they had been there was anybody's guess.

"We've been here almost six minutes," said Heneghan. "Not the brightest bunch of criminals, are you? They only sent two of us, as they say you're museum types who won't put up a fuss."

"Have we done something wrong?" asked Da, befuddled, still on the floor.

"I think you know exactly what you've done, Boyle. Where's the Bog Man? The old mummified geezer?"

In a state of pure shock, Mum and Da led the officers up the narrow stairs to their lab in the attic, where they opened a coffin-shaped crate to reveal . . . nothing. Just a bit of bog goo at the bottom of the crate.

"We've been robbed!" screamed Mum.

"But . . . how?" sputtered Da. "Who knew, except . . ."

"Lord Desmond Dooley!" gasped Mum.

Detective Heneghan collected a dozen of their metal detectors into evidence, along with a shopping bag full of euros—obviously planted. Detective Heneghan told Mum and Da that the garda had been "tipped off" about the Bog Man by a well-connected and reliable source. Of course, it was Lord Desmond Dooley. Later that night, Dooley himself identified them in a lineup. It's madness. The criminal justice system is very much rigged in favor of the rich and powerful.

Mum and Da were taken to Mountjoy to await trial. At this point, I would be remiss if I didn't wonder aloud: *If my parents had truly committed a crime, why would they be at home, playing "Are You There, Moriarty?" and rolling around on the kitchen floor like eejits?* It just doesn't add up. Unless they *are* eejits, which I hope is not true.

On the night of my parents' arrest, I was remanded to the authority of the Department of Children's Services. When there were no other offers, they delivered me into the "care" of Dolores Mullen, my parents' former intern. Dolores was currently living way out west in Galway (and even more currently drinking her second margarita and dancing in our kitchen to Roxy Music like a lunatic). Dolores is a delight. She has a perfectly round face and dyed pink hair and is one of those very few people who can pull off a nose ring. She wears vintage dresses and has a tattoo on her arm of the number forty-two, which is a reference to some book that she loves. Dolores devours books voraciously. I've never actually asked how old Dolores is, as I've been told it's inappropriate to ask this of a lady, but she seems like a very immature late twentysomething. The scandal had kept Dolores out of museum work, and she was now happier, and making a far better income, as a busker* on Shop Street.

---

* Street performer.

A few days after my parents' conviction, I was having my first visit with them. It was a grim Christmas Day in the awfully lit visitors' room at Mountjoy Prison that makes everyone look seasick.

Da passed me a small gift wrapped in toilet paper, the only kind of gift wrap available to inmates. A nearby guard nodded—clearly, they had preapproved this special Christmas transaction with their son.

"Happy Christmas, Ronan," said Da.

"It's not much, just some little somethings. We made them ourselves in the shop," said Mum.

I unwrapped the gift and held in a tiny little scream. They had made me two small clay bookends that were busts of their own heads: one of Mum's face, one of Da's.

"Can you believe we made them ourselves in the prison workshop?" said Da proudly, hugging me close. "They can watch over you even when we can't."

"Say what you want, wrongful imprisonment is truly bringing out the *artistes* in us!" chuckled Mum.

There was no doubt that they had made these little heads themselves. They were meant to be cute but were legitimately unsettling. My parents are curators, not artists. The heads vaguely resembled Mum and Da, but each one was grinning like the Joker, and their little eyes were drifting apart, like a chameleon hunting two different flies.

"Wow. Brilliant" was all I could muster. They beamed—clearly, they were pretty proud of their work. "So, so . . . unlike anything I have. Or have ever seen. Unique indeed."

"They're always protecting you," said Mum with what was meant to be love but felt like a threat. Mum kissed me on the head, and I slipped the scary bookends into my pocket.

"Be careful, son," said Da. "And don't trifle with Lord Desmond Dooley."

I nodded, because I refused to agree to this last part out loud. "I'll be careful, yes," I said, "but I promise you'll never spend another Christmas in Mountjoy Prison."

I headed back to Galway on the 720 Coach, my parents' tiny Joker heads rattling in my pocket. On that ride, I made the vow that I would clear their names. And—if possible— see that Lord Desmond Dooley was put behind bars, even if it meant I had to find the Bog Man myself.

I wasn't sure where to begin on a quest so epic, so I took the first logical step and applied for an internship with the closest available law enforcement agency: the Galway Garda. It turns out this can be done online in just a few minutes.

Captain Fearnley read my application. He was aware of my parents' situation and took pity on me, accepting me even though I was a bit younger than the age requirement for most interns. I'll never know exactly what he said to me on that first day as I sat on his file cabinet and made myself throw up. Even if it was just "Idris Elba, Idris Elba"—that's okay, too. I got the gist. Fearnley would look out for me.

I didn't tell Captain Fearnley that I was joining the garda as part of a plot to exonerate my parents and find a four-thousand-year-old mummy—and there is no place to enter this type of thing in the online application, so I just kept it to myself.

Two years later, back in the present-day shared flat with hilarious Dolores, the sun was starting to set over the bay even though it was not quite four, which is one of the reasons Galway can get melancholy in the wintertime. But Dolores lit the fire and made a pizza topped with leftover wontons that we had in the fridge from Thai takeaway, because Dolores is a genius. Not only a great fiddle player, but the kind of woman unafraid to put leftover wontons on top of a pizza.

A few minutes later, my eyes were swollen shut from either the pizza or the wontons or possibly both. As I have noted, I have many severe allergies.

We sat on the couch, and, in my nearly blinded state, I related to Dolores the bizarre events of the day at Clifden Castle, even though Pat Finch had made me sign a nondisclosure agreement specifically stating that I would not tell anybody anything. This is pretty much the way it works in the world. If you absolutely do want someone to tell other people about something, make them swear that they will not. It's the human way. This is one area where leprechauns have it sorted out.*

Dolores interrogated me for ages—what is a real leprechaun like? Was he cute? Did I find his pot of gold? Did he fill my shoes with candy? Could she *have* some of the

---

* Leprechauns keep their secrets locked in containers they call claddagh jars, and if you open someone else's, you're cursed with an egregious case of diarrhea. Yes, I am aware that this is a disgusting detail, but the wee folk are often vindictive and frightening in their ways, and if you're reading these diaries, you should be forewarned—there will be times when I cannot paint a rosy picture.

candy? These sorts of questions were starting to seem silly to me, as my first encounter with a leprechaun was as much fun as, say, riding a Ferris wheel with a cobra. I told her as much as I knew, which was pitifully little. Neither one of us had ever heard of the Garda Special Unit of Tir Na Nog, as it is an enigmatic organization.

When I ran out of answers, Dolores got her fiddle out. She played until the wee hours, and we wrapped the evening up by singing "The Broad Majestic Shannon," which is a great song.

I awoke on Thursday with my brain spinning like a dreidel about the night ahead.

I checked the coach schedule to calculate how long it would take to get to Killarney. Ireland is a tiny country, but the distances can be exaggerated if you must rely on the coach system.

Dolores was nowhere to be found in the flat, which is

her natural state, as she is quite popular and probably the most fun and unreliable guardian imaginable. I mailed a letter off to my parents in Dublin, relating the news to them and assuring them that I would visit as soon as I could.

CHAPTER FOUR

COLLINS HOUSE

At just noon on Thursday I loaded myself and my duffel bag onto the Number 13 coach from Eyre Square and arrived in Killarney six hours later.

Having no car or license saves me a great deal of stress, as driving in Ireland is a deadly game of chicken in a lush maze with old tractors being driven by farmers who know they are going to heaven when they die, so—watch yerself. Driving on the Emerald Isle is not recommended for the faint of heart.

The offices of the Garda Special Unit of Tir Na Nog are located in the Killarney National Park in an 1830s stone mansion called Collins House. Collins House is large and imposing; it's also enchanted with a spell cast by an old faerie prince named Ciaran the Less Confused. There's a song you must sing to Collins House to be able to see it, and while the song is classified and I will not write it down, I can tell you that it is much longer than you would expect, and the middle part is quite high and tricky. I certainly didn't nail it on my first few tries. If you don't know the song, Collins House just looks like a picnic table.

At 8:45 P.M. I was inside the bustling lobby of the house, addressing a thick and severe desk sergeant named Jeanette O'Brien, who seemed to take an instant disliking to me.

"I'm Ronan Boyle," I explained. "Captain de Valera ordered me to report for the Special Unit."

"And how is this my problem?" Sergeant O'Brien

shouted back at me. "Am I your nanny? I got phones ringing off the hook, Boyle. I got five kids at home with the flu. I got a report of a Dullahan on the N72. Sort yourself out and get a proper uniform if you're going to work here." And with that she thrust her furry paw out at a sign that pointed toward the Supply and Weapons Department.

When I say "paw," I mean that literally, because Sergeant O'Brien is a púca, which is a shape-changing faerie who can sometimes appear to be human and at other times appear to be a cat, goat, rabbit, or horse, among other creatures. I had mistakenly assumed that all of the officers of the Special Unit were human beings, but O'Brien was the first of many faerie folk I would meet at Collins House. For the next twelve weeks, every time I would pass the sergeant's desk, I would note O'Brien in her various púca forms—they change depending on her mood and the temperature. Rabbit O'Brien, whom I had just met, was actually one of her more pleasant manifestations. If you were ever to walk by the desk and see horse O'Brien, or (God forbid) human O'Brien, don't engage—it will not go well.

The hiring of faerie folk by the Special Unit dates all the way back to the mid-1990s, after the unit was involved in a lawsuit brought by two clurichauns, twin brothers named Aodh the Incredibly Clever, and Cian the Less Clever but More Handsome Twin of Aodh.

With the help of a human lawyer in Dublin, their suit stated that the Garda Special Unit of Tir Na Nog was in violation of wee folks' rights by hiring only human beings. The Special Unit lost the lawsuit and subsequently had to hire faerie folk in certain appropriate jobs. It's worth noting that the two clurichauns who filed the lawsuit—Aodh and Cian—were employed for precisely one day in the Donegal office before they robbed the place. When I say "robbed the place," I mean exactly that. They took it. The entire building. Go look for the Donegal office of the Special Unit—*it's not there anymore*. It's not hiding; it's very much gone. Stolen by Aodh and Cian. Remember: Clurichauns are not leprechauns—do not trust them.

POLITE REMINDER!

Information leading to the safe return of the Donegal office of the Garda Special Unit of Tir Na Nog or the whereabouts of the clurichauns Aodh and Cian will be handsomely rewarded.

Finbar Dowd
Deputy Commissioner
Special Unit of Tir Na Nog

I pushed my way through the busy main-floor hallway of Collins House. The walls were crammed with paintings and memorials to various garda officers and faerie folk. From the displays, it became clear to me that the Special Unit was much older than I had thought. Amongst the bric-a-brac were letters, platters, swords, and shillelaghs dating back to the 1700s. The scale of the items was a touch confusing. There was a jewel-encrusted crown almost four feet in diameter hanging next to a shillelagh as small as a toothpick. A few items caught my eye in particular: one was a black-and-white photo of a merrow—a half woman, half seal. She was having a luncheon on a beach with what looked like James Joyce. It was signed at the bottom: "Thanks for the great sandwiches, J.J." The other was a framed platinum record of U2's *Achtung Baby* signed by Larry Mullen Jr., with the inscription "Now I can finally use my chimney again! All the best, Larry."

The Supply and Weapons Department is in the east corner of Collins House next to the astonishingly bad cafeteria. There's a window and a chicken-wire cage with a human attendant named Gary, who looks like he has never been outside in his entire life.

One wall of the S&W Department is a display of supplies available for purchase: knee protectors, torches, gloves, notebooks, pens, rhyming dictionaries, carabiners, etc.

The wall adjacent to it displays weapons: shillelaghs, anti-troll sprays, holy water atomizers, brass knuckles, and various flasks of very good and very bad whiskeys, which can be used to reward or trick at least seventy-five percent of land-based faerie folk.

Gary was being assisted by Dan, a one-eyed bridge troll

in a lavender jumpsuit, because some nonviolent prisoners from the Joy Vaults are allowed to do work-release programs in garda offices around the country.

I explained to pale Gary that I was a new trainee, and I had been told to collect a uniform. I'd be lying if I didn't tell you I was pretty excited about the prospect of a new outfit, especially since currently I was in my backup garda uniform trousers, which were ever-so-slightly too snug.

I pictured myself in a slick version of Captain de Valera's rig—the leather boots, the gloves, the knee protectors—but alas, my hopes were dashed. Dan the Troll climbed up to a very high shelf—apparently this was his job—and returned with my temporary uniform: navy blue overalls with rubber kneepads and the word TRAINEE on the back in reflective print. Where my badge would be was just a patch.

I was issued a new torch, a flask of the worst available whiskey, and an entry-level shillelagh made from hemlock, too light to inflict any real damage, but perhaps this was the point. I gave it a few practice twirls and lost hold of it. It rattled across the linoleum floor, to my embarrassment.

Dan the Troll blinked his singular eye and pointed to a sign on the wall that read: IS YOUR SHILLELAGH SECURE?

Pale Gary gave me a small map of the house and the Trainee's Handbook, and then a bill for six euros, which is what the Trainee's Handbook costs. He directed me to the barracks, which are in the attic of Collins House.

There is a lift* in the house, but I would never recommend using it in a zillion years if you have my fear of confined spaces or body odor. The lift dates from the 1930s and is excruciatingly slow. It always smells of a strange mix of coffee, stressed-out humans, and curious faerie aromas. I would hate to be trapped in that lift in the event of an emergency, and so I always take the stairs—which are a stone spiral set, seven stories up, and lit by oil lamps, as the stone walls are too thick for electrical wires. While the stairs are cramped and mildewy, they don't rely on ancient pulleys like the frightening lift does.

The barracks is a very fancy name for the actual room

---

* Elevator.

that trainees and cadets occupy in Collins House. In reality, it's just a dusty attic with discarded sofas and cots radiating out from an old potbelly stove. I tossed my new handbook down on an empty cot close to the stove and kicked off my trainers. I closed my eyes in an attempt to rest my brain, which was overinflated with new information. A few minutes later I was awakened with the not-so-gentle thump of a boot to my temple.

"Oi, noobster,"* said a scratchy voice. Three seniors were scowling down at me. The leader of the group was Big Jimmy Gibbons, the sweatiest person I have ever met. Honestly, I have no idea why his nickname isn't "Sweaty Jimmy"—because he's not even that big. His sweatiness and his nastiness are his most defining traits.

"Stove cots ain't for noobsters, ya daft noobster," said Jimmy with a voice that was ruined at some point in his life and now sounded like someone dragging a canoe across gravel.

Turns out the cots closest to the stove are reserved for

---

* *Noobster* is the slang term for new recruits.

the senior recruits. This is what Big Sweaty Jimmy Gibbons was trying to explain to me in the most violent way possible. This is his style. His two henchmen, Dirk Brennan and Chip Flanagan, hoisted me up by the ankles, and I was now dangling like a piñata that no child would want. Big Sweaty Jimmy gave a short, hard punch to the soft part of my middle, knocking the wind out of me.

"Sorry . . . I didn't know," I said as best I could without any air in my system.

"Shut up, noobster," snorted Chip Flanagan. Big Sweaty Jimmy pulled back for another punch, but just then he froze. His eyes glazed over, and remarkably, he began to levitate.

Dirk and Chip gasped and dropped me on the top of my skull. I looked up to see that Big Sweaty Jimmy wasn't actually floating. He was being held aloft by the waistband of his underpants. His scream would have woken the dead, had he not ruined his voice at some point in the past. But this was no ordinary wedgie happening to Big Sweaty Jimmy Gibbons—he was three full feet off the ground. Who—or what—in the world had that kind of strength?

Log MacDougal. Log has that kind of strength. She can hold a full-grown man in an airborne wedgie for as long as she wants. Her arm was chiseled like some kind of over-the-top statue of Zeus.

"Let the noobster be, or I'll eat your face," giggled Log MacDougal, an insane glint in her eyes.

Log MacDougal is six feet tall. She has bleached white hair, a nose that seems to have been broken a dozen times, and the strength of a chimpanzee. She has the nervous habit of laughing under her breath both while awake and while asleep, which can give the impression that she is a psychopath, which she in fact may be. At this point, Log had repeated the trainee program four times without ever graduating.

With a tragic snap of elastic, Log MacDougal dropped Big Sweaty Jimmy to the floor. Jimmy's pride would never quite recover, and this pair of underwear would never be wearable again. Not by him, anyway.

Jimmy, Dirk, and Chip scampered off down the spiral staircase as fast as they could, which was a bad idea, as the

stairs are often slick. I could hear them slipping and falling for a surprisingly long time.

Log hoisted me up. She leaned in close, her cheek next to mine. It seemed like she was going to whisper a secret in my ear. She did not.

She just giggled.

Log MacDougal would take some getting used to.

Being a brand-noobster, I would occupy the worst cot, farthest from the potbelly stove and closest to the bathroom, which everyone calls the loo. The attic has no windows. The instructors say that this is a great way to adjust to the nocturnal schedule of the Special Unit, but it's really just an excuse for why there is no view, when one of Lough Leane would be spectacular from this height.

After a fitful non-sleep, I got up that afternoon and put on my new trainee jumpsuit. I was pleased to find it didn't look all that terrible. It fit my small frame relatively well and was warm and comfortable, allowing for great freedom of movement—like a pair of battle pajamas.

I attached my torch and flask to the utility belt and practiced trying to lock the shillelagh into the hooks on my back. It turns out this is much harder than Captain de Valera had made it look at Clifden Castle. Basically, you have to use your shoulder as a lever and smack it with the shillelagh just right to get it to lock into place. After three failed attempts, I rested the shillelagh between my back and the wall and forced it into the hooks with the weight of my body. I'm glad nobody saw me do this.

The first day for all trainees at Collins House is called "Frolic Day," and it lives up to the name. At dusk, to the ear-destroying drone of bagpipes, the trainees line up in the courtyard. Four of us stood there at attention, awaiting the ceremony, while the horrible Pat Finch played "Fields of Athenry" on the pipes. Certain people in this world can play the bagpipes with a light and casual confidence that makes it look ever so easy. Pat Finch is not one of those people. His bagpiping is legitimately scary. The whole time it looked like his eyeballs were about to pop out. Or perhaps he had somehow passed gas in reverse. I couldn't keep watching, and yet I could not look away.

"You're Boyle, right?" said a voice that sounds like what a strawberry milkshake tastes like.

The proprietor of this voice was the trainee to my right: Dermot Lally. Dermot has broad shoulders, a square jaw, and curly black hair and would by any human conventional standards be described as a "dreamboat." He is so much taller than me that he would have blocked out the sun if the sun had been out, which it seldom is in Ireland at this time of year.

Dermot had failed out of military flight school because his vision was not perfect.* In an effort to improve Dermot's vision, he is required to wear an eye patch over his left eye—his is made from white silk and somehow only makes him that much dreamier.

---

* The Special Unit has more stringent smelling tests than vision tests—oftentimes even a hawk can't see the wee folk, as they are so quick, but you can almost always smell them.

"I signed up for the adventure, the mischief, bodily harm, and possibly an early death. But if I'd been told we'd have to listen to the bagpipes—I'd have skipped it," said Dermot, winking his one visible eye.

If you were ever to make a film of my life, I certainly hope you would cast Dermot Lally as Ronan Boyle. In many ways, he's the more cinema-ready version of me. I'd like to tell you that after Frolic Day, Dermot Lally and I forged a lasting friendship, as I have certainly tried to forge one, but to this day he seems to think my name is Little Rick. Where he got this idea, I do not know.

The trainee to my left stuck out his hand. At first, I thought he was having an asthma attack, but he was actually beat-boxing, and—even more surprisingly—he was amazing at it.

"*Allow me to introduce myself, my name is Brian. B to the R-ian,*" he rapped. "*They call me the notorious Brian Bean. Bagged groceries at SuperValu like you've never seen. I murder at rhymes, and you can probably tell that I grew up in Meath, in the hood they call Kells.*"

Then he made the sound of a crowd cheering and flash-bulbs popping. And it was absolutely brilliant.

This was my introduction to the hilarious Brian Bean. Brian Bean can impersonate anyone or anything. His ears poke out like pretzels, and his face turns bright pink when he breaks out into voices that can turn any room into a comedy club. He can mimic the voice of any singer, movie star, footballer—even the sounds of birds, guitars, different types of cars, airplanes, and toaster ovens. He can make himself sound like an old-fashioned phonograph and perform entire radio plays with a dozen characters.

"Wow. Brilliant. Pleased to meet you, Brian. I'm Ronan Boyle," I said, shaking his hand vigorously.

"Actually, I believe *I'm* Ronan Boyle," replied Brian Bean, pushing up imaginary glasses on his nose and doing the most accurate impression of me that nobody on earth had ever seen until now. It was like listening to a mirror. I laughed hard, letting out a snort. The air from my nose fogged up my glasses, which is something that happens.

This was ill-timed, as Captain de Valera was just coming out of Collins House with two dozen officers and the faculty following her. She gave me a biff on the head with her shillelagh. I straightened up.

Next to Brian was the slightly scary Log MacDougal, who had saved me from Big Sweaty Jimmy Gibbons in the barracks. She rocked left and right between her feet, maintaining a low, breathy chuckle. It looked like she was about to take off running, or perhaps launch herself straight up into the air. If I am being honest, Log MacDougal did not seem "functional" in the classic sense of the word.

At the end of the line was a trainee who was never formally introduced to me, but I know his name to be Tim the Medium-Sized Bear. Tim is a medium-sized bear, and honestly, he is a bit of a mystery. He doesn't wear the trainee jumpsuit, just his own bear fur, and he keeps to himself mostly.

As "Fields of Athenry" faded on the pipes, Pat Finch

tipped backward and collapsed. This frightened the rabbit version of Sergeant O'Brien, who shape-shifted into her donkey form, which was interesting to see. She bucked and darted off into the fields toward the lake.

A moment passed, and everyone wondered if their hearing would ever return to normal.

"Céad míle fáilte," said Deputy Commissioner Finbar Dowd into an old-fashioned megaphone. "A hundred thousand welcomes to Collins House." Finbar Dowd is a man so overwhelmingly ordinary that he defies description. Picture him in your head. There! You did it. No matter what you pictured, you are correct. That's him.

Dowd gestured up to the coat of arms above the front doors, which depicted a shillelagh violently cracking a leprechaun on the skull with the Latin words PUGNABIMUS NYMPHARUM across it. The leprechaun's eyes were replaced with Xs—either to symbolize that he was drunk or that the crack to his skull had killed him.

"Yes, many people, especially in this era, have

complained about the insensitive coat of arms," continued Dowd.* "Please, no more emails about the coat of arms. And if you're already on the email chain, please don't 'reply all.' There is a committee looking into some new coat of arms designs, and I assure you, we're taking everyone's point of view into account," droned the astonishingly ordinary Finbar Dowd. He opened up an old scroll, which was an awkward moment, as he wasn't sure what to do with the megaphone in his other hand. Perhaps Sergeant O'Brien was supposed to hold it, but she was now a donkey, rubbing her behind against a low stone wall and really enjoying it.

"Professor Wise Young Jim of the Honey Caves shall now read the Recruit's Pledge, and yes, there will be a test on it later," said Dowd.

A fourteen-hundred-year-old leprechaun named Wise Young Jim of the Honey Caves waddled forward and took the scroll. Wise Young Jim is three feet tall, but his beard is

---

* *Hello. Finbar Dowd, Deputy Commissioner here in the footnotes. This is one of my rare appearances in Ronan Boyle's diaries, which is surprising, as I am a major figure in the Special Unit and well-liked at Collins House.*

twenty-seven feet long. He pushes it around in front of him in a wheelbarrow. He took a short pull on a flask and began to read the pledge.

"In rain, in mist, or light to medium fog, in drizzle, or just a sprinkling, or even proper bucketing, or if it's pissing, or really pelting down, we still go out. Go out and get 'em. If . . . of course . . . we can get 'em. God knows we try. Try . . . try for sure. Special Unit . . . number one, whoo," said Wise Young Jim, and then he burped.

This is *word for word* the Recruit's Pledge, even though it sounded like he was making it up on the spot. I read the scroll in the library, and this is exactly the way it's written. Even with the pauses and the burp at the end. So, so strange. And almost impossible to repeat, which is what we had to do right then and there. It took a lot of tries. Then there was also a written test on it, right on the spot. Everyone failed the test, but luckily we would be tested on the pledge every single day in Wise Young Jim's class, so there would be many more chances to get it right.

After the pledge, a marvelous picnic luncheon and

boating trip was held for the new recruits, out on Lough Leane. The lunch included creamy leek and potato soup, curried chicken salad sandwiches on toasted sourdough baguette, and a type of homemade potato crisp dusted with dill and sea salt that remain the finest crisps I've ever had to this very day.

After everyone had eaten as much as they could, the trainees were handed all of their course books for the twelve-week program. Then, two seconds later, the boat was set on fire by the graduating trainees, who shot burning arrows at it from the shoreline. This "escape a boat that's on fire" bit was the big, not-so-fun surprise of the very inaccurately named Frolic Day.

The new recruits—now stuffed to the gills with curried chicken salad—had to escape a burning boat and swim back half a kilometer to land while keeping all of their new books dry. Honestly, if Log MacDougal hadn't towed me the last hundred meters, I very likely would have drowned.

Brian Bean did drown. This is the big test of Frolic Day—surviving it.

Later that night, I shivered in my cot, half-watching Dermot Lally in his extensive bedtime preparations that included a Moroccan hair oil treatment, slathering his face with petroleum jelly, and putting on strange mitts for his hands, designed to keep them as soft as a baby's behind.

"Must take care of your skin, Little Rick. It's your biggest organ," said Dermot, who had taken off his eye patch to sleep. The "Little Rick" confusion was compounded by the fact that my trainee jumpsuit had stitching that literally said RONAN BOYLE over the left breast pocket. Perhaps Dermot could not read? But then why was he so confident? It was confounding.

I was feeling pretty low and a bit lonely, even in the crowded, smelly barracks. I missed my parents. I had the little clay busts they had made me on a shelf above my cot. (Big Sweaty Jimmy Gibbons had asked why I had lizards watching me, and it was a fair question.) I missed Dolores, as unreliable as she is. And though I'd only known him for an hour, the death of Brian Bean bothered me a little bit.

On the bed next to mine, Log was softly giggling, as is her custom. With a switchblade, she carved something into the leg of her cot.

Tim the Medium-Sized Bear was curled up asleep right next to the potbelly stove. This is a breach of protocol for a new trainee, but it seems the senior recruits were willing to give him a pass, as he is not a small bear.

I flipped through my course books, which were mostly dry, except for a few mushy pages in the back of *Tin Whistle for Beginners*. Sensing my sad mood, Log shot her crazy eyes in my direction. (Have you ever tried to set something on fire with your mind? That's what it looks like when Log looks right at you.)

"You want to hear a song that the otters sing, Boyle?" she giggled.

"The others or the otters?"

"Aye, the otters. It'll cheer you up, lad. That's what it's for."

"Um. Sure. I suppose?"

I took Log to mean a song about otters. But no, this was a song by otters. She popped her two front teeth out over her lip and began whistling and clicking in a way that was both genuinely delightful and quite mental. I couldn't help but snort, fogging up my glasses.

"Brilliant. Did you just make that up?" I asked.

"No, I just told you," chuckled Log. "That was taught to me by an otter named Quick Ronnie. It's actually a very dirty song. He taught it to me in Tir Na Nog."

I sat up on my cot like I'd just been hit by lightning. "Wait, you've actually been to Tir Na Nog? The land of the faeries?"

Log burst out laughing, which made everyone in the barracks give a little jump. Her chimpanzee strength, short temper, and her reputation as someone not to be trifled with were now well established.

"I haven't just been to Tir Na Nog, Boyle," whispered Log, leaning in close. "I'm *from* Tir Na Nog."

My mouth went slack. "Seriously . . . how?"

"I was a changeling, Ronan. Raised in Tir Na Nog by leprechauns."

I looked down to see that what she had been carving

into the post of her cot was the very realistic face of a human baby.

"That's how I learned the language of the animals. As an infant, I was stolen and replaced by a changeling. But they forgot that they stole me, and for a couple of years the wee folk thought I was just a lifelike log, and so they raised me as one. That's why I go by Log, and not my real name, Lara."

"Mistaken for a log? But how could that even happen?" I asked.

"Sure, seems impossible to you. But the wee folk drink way too much, and this kind of thing happens all the time. One of me mates back then when I was a log in Tir Na Nog was just a pile of cabbages that a wee man had taught how to dance with some kind of spell. He was the best student in class. His name might have been Ronan also. Trying to remember. No, now that I think of it, we just called him Pile of Cabbages."

"So, wait, how did you end up here?" I asked, my brain quietly exploding in my head.

"The human Republic had an amnesty treaty with the

wee folk a while back to return changelings that had been stolen. As part of it, the humans are obliged to help us 'changies' find decent jobs. I worked at the Department of Transport, Tourism, and Sport before coming here, but I wasn't a good fit for desk work, and I kept throwing people at things. Especially right before lunch."

"Ah, I see. Wow. That's quite a story, Log. I mean—Lara, or I mean . . . Which do you prefer?"

"I like you, Boyle. But never, ever call me Lara, or I'll eat your face," said Log, as sincerely as anyone has ever said anything to me, while tapping me lightly on the nose with the tip of her switchblade.

Despite appearances, Log is actually very intense. Best not to ever look at her funny, make any sudden movements, or cross her in even the most minor way. Or call her by her human name of Lara. She will also take anything of yours that's not nailed down. She can't help it—the poor girl was raised as a log. Also, as I mentioned, she laughs under her breath while awake and asleep, which is very unsettling. That said, if I had to pick any of the trainees to be on my side in a fight, it would certainly be Log MacDougal. And also, she would probably be the one who started that fight, because she has major rage issues, drinks like a leprechaun, and loves to make rude jokes.

When I awoke that afternoon, I could feel that my nose was getting stuffed up, and perhaps I was coming down with a cold after all of the shivering I did on Frolic Day. My new friend Log came to my rescue yet again.

"Want to know how the wee folk fight off a cold?" she asked with a sly wink and the low, insane chuckle that accompanied everything she said.

"Um . . . yes?" I replied.

And with that Log licked her finger, stuck it into my belly button, and slapped me across the face with my own shoe. Then she laughed like this was the funniest thing that had ever happened. Remember, Log was raised as a log, and sometimes she doesn't know any better. But I should add I was so confused that I immediately became flushed and sweaty, and whether it was the sheer annoyance or the boost of endorphins, I actually did feel much better ten minutes later, with zero symptoms of a cold. So, while possibly a legitimate psychopath, Log isn't always wrong.

Trainees must complete four courses to qualify for cadet, which is the first rank of the Special Unit. Cadet is followed by detective, sergeant, lieutenant, captain, and commissioner. The classes are: Weaponized Poetry, Shillelagh Safety and Combat, Practices of Irish and Faerie Law, and Tin Whistle for Beginners. Honestly, Tin Whistle for Beginners is probably the hardest of the four, and it's only required because certain faerie folk in the Undernog— the southernmost tip of Tir Na Nog—speak using only tin whistles. It's a pleasant but grueling language to learn. Luckily, trainees are only required to play a few dozen basic phrases like "Do you understand your Republic rights?" and "Help, I am lost in Undernog."

At dawn on my second day at Collins House, my first Shillelagh Safety and Combat class began with zero warning when someone kicked over my cot and dumped a can of Schweppes on my face.

"What is the opposite of failure, Boyle?" asked Yogi

Hansra as she choked me with an advanced type of double shillelagh she carries that looks like nunchucks—two short shillelaghs connected by a chain. It allows for amazing 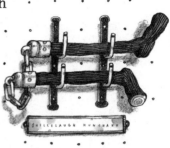 speed and fancy moves. It's also perfect for simply choking a trainee in an attic, as she was doing right now.

Yogi Hansra is four feet, ten inches tall. She might have the most magnificent head of blue-black hair, but we will never know because she keeps it buzzed short. She is quite pretty and probably would have been a star in the Bollywood film industry if she had not been called to a life of whacking the daylights out of people with sticks.

"Um . . . The opposite of failure is success?" I sputtered. "Right?"

"Wrong, Boyle! The opposite of failure is *readiness*." With that, she leaped up and landed in a rather spectacular split, her bare feet far apart, holding her on two beams that support the roof. She twirled her nunchuck-shillelaghs until they were only a blur. I did the kind of stupid thing Ronan Boyle does.

I applauded.

This was a weird move, but it just happened. Her eyes tightened, and I got the point: This wasn't a performance; it was a fight. I rubbed my throat and grabbed my training shillelagh from under my cot as she leaped toward me, driving me backward down the spiral staircase with a dizzying series of whacks.

"I'm Yogi Hansra, your Shillelagh Safety and Combat teacher, Mr. Boyle," said the yogi. "When you're in my class, check your attitude at the door. Shoes are okay but not preferred; if you have to go to the bathroom, just go, you don't have to ask permission. There's no such thing as a dumb question. If you don't understand something, raise your hand."

"Um. Okay." I stopped fighting and raised my hand.

The yogi bowed and rested her shillechucks on her hip.

"*Namaste*, Mr. Boyle," she said. "That means 'I bow to you.'"

"Oh. Okay. Sure. Neat," I said, bowing back at her and gasping for air. "And when, exactly, is shillelagh class? I didn't see it on my schedule."

"Shillelagh class is always happening. It's happening right now. In the future. In the distant past," said the yogi without trying to be funny. "Or possibly it's never happening, because where we live is a construct of the mind. The only real thing is the breath. Understand?"

"No, ma'am," I said genuinely.

"You will understand, Boyle. I promise you will understand. Now, what is the only real thing?"

"The breath?"

"Good. Because we may exist in a . . . ?"

"Construct of the mind?"

"Excellent."

She spun her shillechucks around her body as she whacked and chased me down the hall and through the astonishingly bad cafeteria. The tables were crowded, but nobody even looked up. Apparently, this was a normal type of occurrence with the yogi. Eventually I made it to the basement and eluded her long enough to hide in a large dryer in the laundry cave. I waited almost an hour to be sure that she was gone. When I climbed out, I was covered in a copious amount of lint. I don't know if my shillelagh class was over, because to quote the yogi herself, "Class is always happening, or maybe it's never happening." I was very confused.

The yogi's class was different every day. Monday, you climb a very tall tree, and you can't come down until you've written a letter to yourself in the future. Tuesday, you balance on a fence post for many hours while she throws plates at you. Often there is real shillelagh fighting against the yogi, yet many more days are devoted only to breathing. The only thing about her class that can be expected is the unexpected. And of course—the breathing stuff. So much breathing stuff.

If you're wondering why the yogi is so intense, perhaps it's because of her complicated life story: She was born in Mumbai, India, in 1989. At age six, she began working for a medicine man who would perform "brain surgery" on her in public squares. Really he was just pulling a bunch of spinach rigatoni out of her ear. She was rescued by the monks of the Boudhanath Temple, who smuggled her to Nepal. Every day, she tried to escape from the monks using the only things she could find, which were often just sticks or her own elbows. She battled dozens of annoyed monks every day until they just gave up and let her go. The short version: Do not mess with Yogi Hansra. She loves to fight. She also teaches an amazing hot yoga class at Collins House, Mondays and Fridays at two P.M. Bring lots of water. Her motto, "The Opposite of Failure Is Readiness," can be purchased on tank tops she sells after class, but they're not as popular as the ones that say "Sometimes Karma Comes on a Stick."

Weaponized Poetry—my best subject—is taught outdoors in an obstacle course in Killarney National Park. The instructor is Pat Finch, the single most horrible man on the island of Ireland. The class is exactly what it sounds like: coming up with rhymes in confusing situations. The most stressful of the obstacles are the Buttered Wall (self-explanatory) and something called Pig Maze.

"Why is it called Pig Maze, sir?" I dared to ask Pat Finch as we stood at a heavy wooden gate, him scratching his belly underneath his belt with an old fork.

It was a rare sunny day in Killarney, which made Pat Finch look more out of place than normal, as his face is like something you'd expect to see peeking out of a coffin.

He responded in classic Pat Finch style by plugging one nostril and blowing snot onto the ground. "Grab a belt and put 'em on, noobsters. See you on the other side. Or maybe not."

Pat Finch approached the gate that leads into the maze itself, a labyrinth of hedges four square kilometers wide.

Dan the Troll passed out the belts, which were really just rope strung with cinnamon-flavored apples. He tied them onto our waists, tight. Pat Finch took several minutes to climb up into the crow's nest, which is a sort of lookout tower above the maze.

Dan the Troll opened the gate and ushered us into the maze, bolting it behind us.

"Maybe the apples are a treat? They do smell awfully good," I said, bending down to try to lick one of them and immediately getting a cramp in my side.

Log giggled, but in her most serious way. This was her fifth time through the trainee program. She knew the apples weren't for us.

When pigs arrived, I understood the name of the maze. A dozen of the largest, friendliest pigs you've ever seen in your entire life were barreling down on us. These pigs really want to get a bite of those apples and to snuggle. Snuggling a four-hundred-pound pig—even a friendly one—would be painful and possibly fatal.

Everyone scattered in different directions as I let out one of my famous Ronan Boyle shrieks. A few turns later, I ran dead-end into a gate, which, after a furtive panic, I realized could only be raised from above—by Pat Finch, up in the crow's nest, with a set of block-and-tackle pulleys like you might see on an old ship.

"Rhyme time, ya dirty eejit!" Finch shouted at me from above.

Next to the gate was a bowl filled with cards. I pulled one out and read it. The question written on it was: "How can I marry Margaret—you know she's made of concrete and marzipan?"

I could hear the friendly pigs just a few turns behind me. The upbeat snorting and thumping of hooves was intense. Up above, Pat Finch fired off a starter pistol—not to symbolize the start of anything, just to add to the chaos.

I had already forgotten the question. I had to reread it, wasting precious seconds. Three of the pigs rounded the corner straight toward me. They were so close, I could feel their hot breath. The largest, cutest one of them got a bite of a belt apple and pulled me down. Their friendliness was overwhelming. I pounded on the gate.

"Finch, please!" I cried.

But Pat Finch was now tuning up his bagpipes. If you don't love bagpipes, you *really* won't love the sound of them being tuned up. Between the blaring pipes, the pig snorts, and my adrenaline pumping, the Pig Maze was now an absolute disaster on all fronts.

Without thinking, I blurted out the best rhyme I could

come up with to match the question on the card: "Come on, let's play some darts, quick. I'm going to use my bare feet if I can."

Up in the nest, Pat Finch rang a bell, which meant that my rhyme was sufficient. He pulled a lever, and the gate popped open. I dove through to the other side. The gate snapped down behind me, and I could hear the wonderful pigs bumping against it and then doubling back to hunt me down again. I remembered something somebody once said about always going left in a maze to find your way out. I can't say if this is true or not, as after six or so left turns I was still very stuck. I finally encountered Log and Dermot running toward me, the full complement of cheerful pigs right behind them.

At this point I wondered: Where was Tim the Medium-Sized Bear? He hardly ever showed up for classes, and in the maze he could have been a real asset.

It was a hundred meters to the next gate. Up above, Pat Finch was attempting to play "Sweet Child o' Mine" on the bagpipes, and it sounded like a cat being declawed inside a set of bagpipes. We reached the gate, and Log grabbed a card, studying it for a long time.

"What does it say? Hurry, Log! Please!" I yelled. "Whatever you've got!"

"Sorry, lads, I forgot that I can't read human. No wonder I never pass these classes," said Log, shrugging and handing me the card.

I read it aloud. It was an obscure question that surely has never been uttered by a real person in English. It read: "When is the rent due for your pied-à-terre?"

Above us, Pat Finch fired off a few more shots from the starter pistol and then bagpiped like someone who had *not* made a deal with the devil. The pigs closed in on Dermot Lally, knocking him down and swarming him with their affection. They licked his face and devoured every last one of his belt apples.

Glancing at the card, I yelped out, "Let's glue some tin cans to Fred's derrière!"

Derrière means *bottom.** It was a tacky rhyme, obviously, and I'm not proud of it, but Dermot was about to be snuggled

---

* Bottom means *butt.*

to death, so I took a chance. Finch considered the rhyme for longer than seemed fair, then rang the bell and pulled the lever.

I pushed Log out the gate and yanked Dermot through behind me. We had made it out the other side of the maze. Dan the Troll slammed the bolt to the wooden gate, sealing off the ever-so-friendly pigs.

Dermot and I tumbled to the ground, laughing, and I felt for certain that he and I would now be mates. He hoisted me up and tossed me in the air like a baby, which was odd and, honestly, somewhat fun. I thoroughly enjoyed the moment, right up until he clapped me on the back and said, "Thanks, Little Rick—you're a champ."

Again, I have no idea why he thinks my name is Little Rick, other than the letter *R* having a leading role in both.

Wise Young Jim, our Practices of Irish and Faerie Law teacher, started each of his classes with the Recruit's Pledge, which was too vague to remember but has something to do with not being afraid of six types of rain, and then you have to do a burp at the end of it.

"When I was your age, a millennium and a half ago, nobody just handed us careers like they do now," said Young Jim to us in his seemingly endless first lecture, which was mostly his own life story. "I could have been an actor in Tir Na Nog, but that racket is all about who you know. Not talent. 'Kiss up to the big shots, Young Jim,' 'Make sure you mingle with the casting agents, Young Jim,' 'Send out solstice presents with your new headshots on them, Young Jim.' Nowadays you can just film yerself doing jumping jacks in yer knickers on a mobile phone, and next day you're a household name! Fie!!!"

Wise Young Jim's lecture was so epically dull that, fortyish minutes in, even he fell asleep, quietly face-planting into the wheelbarrow that transports his beard. Log quietly piled up some extra beard around him, like tucking a baby bird into a nest, motioning for us to sneak out after her.

As Collins House turned back into a picnic table, Log led us south through the forest toward the Upper Lake. Tim the Medium-Sized Bear was accompanying us, or perhaps he was just following us. It's hard to tell with him sometimes.

"Who wants to play hide-and-seek?" asked Log in a low chuckle. For some reason Log can make a sentence this innocent sound mischievous.

"Sure," I replied, unaware that Log only plays the leprechaun version of hide-and-seek, which is epic.

Dermot Lally was declared "it," and Log grabbed my hand and ran with me while Dermot counted to thirty-four-hundred (leprechaun rules). I thought for sure we were about to be busted, as Sergeant O'Brien trotted toward us in the form of a fox, but it turned out to be an actual fox. Log consulted with her in the language of the animals, then led us up a stream to cover our scent. We must have run for three kilometers. Then Log painstakingly crafted two life-sized dummies of us out of sticks and hay. She then marked the dummies with a small jar of fox urine she had purchased from the fox to further confuse anyone seeking us. At the bank of a stream, she showed me how to become invisible just using mud and leaves. We slopped the mud all over us until nothing but our eyes were visible. Then we rolled in the leaves, closed our eyes, and crouched in the embankment.

Twelve hours passed.

Neither Dermot nor Tim the Medium-Sized Bear ever found us. Log laughed hard, as this meant that we had won! Sure. We had won?

I had a nose blocked with mud and could not feel either of my legs. Back at Collins House that morning, even the huevos rancheros in the astonishingly bad cafeteria tasted good to me.

Tin Whistle for Beginners is by far the hardest class at Collins House. The instructor is recognizable as one of the Clancy Brothers, or maybe he is a dead ringer for one of the Clancy Brothers. Or possibly Spider Stacy from the Pogues. He definitely has an interesting hat, and I'm certain I know his face from somewhere. Unfortunately, I had taken a bad fall on the Butter Wall and was out with a sprained neck on the first day of class and never caught his name. Any questions in his class must be posed using the tin whistle, so I was never able to ask his name, as that would be a very advanced question for a beginner. Now it's ages later and

feels inappropriate to ask his name—it would just be so embarrassing for both of us. In the halls of Collins House, I simply say, "Hello, guy" whenever I see him, and he points and says, "There's a fellow," and this vague repartee seems to suffice for us. He can certainly play a tin whistle like a madman, whoever he is. It may come to me in a moment.

CHAPTER FIVE
EXAMS

eek twelve of the training program
is exams and happened to fall
right before the Faerie New Year.*
In Tin Whistle for Beginners,

---

* The Spring Solstice, 21 March, is New Year's Day for the faerie folk. It's
a busy day for the Special Unit, as the wee folk make merry, and more than
a few of them end up in custody after crashing stolen pigs that they know
perfectly well they are too inebriated to ride. Later, I would make a series of
public service announcements for the wee folk about the dangers of drinking and riding pigs, starring my friend Aileen, Whose Luscious Eyes Sparkle
Like Ten Thousand Emeralds in the Sun.

For those keeping track of the wee folks' calendar—you would be fools, as
there are no clocks or calendars in Tir Na Nog. Time is a constraint that you
and I understand. The wee folk marvel at our obsession with time, and they
attribute it to the fact that we live such short lives in comparison to theirs.
Have you ever been told about how a housefly lives for just one week? That's
how it feels to leprechauns when they hear that we only live to ninetyish.
It makes them sad, and then it makes them laugh, because they drink too
much, and pretty much everything makes them laugh.

we were required to play questions or statements that we pulled at random from the interesting hat of the instructor whose name escapes me. The one I had to play was "Let me go; I have other humans who will come looking for me if I don't report in on the hour." This is a massive sentence to play, especially if, like Ronan Boyle, you have not been practicing. It felt particularly unfair, as some trainees, like the all-around teacher's pet and dreamboat Dermot Lally, were lucky enough to get "Good morning!" which is just three notes.

The idea of having to use this sentence in the Undernog made me a bit uneasy. What on earth is happening down there? According to my test results, I actually played the statement: "Hold on to my foot; I'm going to frighten the mayor." I received a D-minus, which is the lowest passing grade, and that was only because my tone was "decent."

Yogi Hansra's exam never came, which was the most surprising thing she could do, and a perfect example of her method. When anyone asked when we were to be tested, her response was "When you least expect it."

Tim the Medium-Sized Bear was absent for the

entire week of exams. When I asked about it, everyone just shrugged, which is part of my theory that Tim the Medium-Sized Bear was never a trainee at all—just a regular bear that wandered into Collins House and settled into one of the cots. Neither Sergeant O'Brien nor Captain de Valera seemed to even be aware of any bear trainee, which also supports this "random bear" theory. I asked Log about it, because she and Tim seemed close, but she just giggled, because she is slightly insane.

Graduation day is a twenty-four-hour event at the house called Torture Tuesday. The trainees do not sleep and are given grueling final tests by Sergeant O'Brien. Luckily for me, she was in the form of a goat for my finals, which happens to be her most pleasant manifestation. Other than her chewing on my jumpsuit a bit, I did well and got out of the Pig Maze and up the Butter Wall in record time.

Shockingly, Log passed all of her exams on this, her fifth attempt. When she heard the news that she'd made cadet, she threw her arms around me and wept. It was a rare tender moment from the otherwise tough-as-nails Log MacDougal.

"I wish me wee little mum and tiny da could see me now," said Log with tears rolling down the broken zigzag of her nose and off the side of her face, which is the direction her nose points.

"Well, I'm here, and I'm proud of you, Log," I said as I held her and rocked her gently until I started to see stars, then blacked out completely. Log has the strength of a chimpanzee, and she had accidentally hugged me into a brief coma. This happens sometimes.

We were sent to collect our new uniforms in the Supply and Weapons Department from pale Gary and Dan the Troll. Dan the Troll was leaving, as he had served his time and been paroled.*

The cadet uniform is an olive houndstooth tweed and Kevlar jacket with black knee-length pants and whack

---

* I would meet Dan the Troll again three months later when he was captured after devouring two badly behaved children on a field trip in the lovely town of Cong. But Dan the Troll always lands on his enormous feet, and the schoolteacher leading the field trip even testified on his behalf—seems that these two kids were real eejits. Trolls eating children is really just nature's lint catcher—filtering out some of the ones that shouldn't get through.

guards that run from the shoe up to the knee. The jacket has a thick leather patch to protect the shoulder when flipping your shillelagh on and off and a belt with extra slots for the poetry notebook and the three weaponized whiskeys that cadets must carry. There is also an optional beret that I happen to like very much. With the accessory belt, the whole thing costs 280 euros, but it also comes with terrible complimentary socks that refuse to stay up. The new outfit was fun to wear and looked especially good on Dermot Lally, as his white eye patch can pull whole ensembles together. Somehow Dermot's version of the outfit included a scarf—which is neither allowed nor available in the S&W Department. This was puzzling and maddening.

That night was the graduation céilí, which is held outdoors with all ranks of the Special Unit and is a fine time indeed. Log looked striking in her cadet uniform, her massive biceps almost popping through the tweed. Many toasts were made, and a brief tribute was held for the late, hilarious Brian Bean, the trainee who had perished on Frolic Day and whose ghost had been seen haunting

Collins House on three separate occasions, still doing voices and impressions. The living Brian Bean had been a riot, but when I later encountered his ghost in the library doing an impression of the singer Nicki Minaj, it was a vision so horrifying that I knew I could never unsee it.

"*Boy toy named Troy used to live in Detroit,*" Brian's ghost rapped at me, in the absolutely perfect voice of Nicki Minaj.

"Oh. Hey, Brian," I said politely, but really wishing he'd let me get back to my book. "Great seeing you, mate. I wish we could hang out and I didn't have all this recreational reading looming over me." I rubbed my temples with a pretend headache.

"Oh, sure. Cheers, Ronan," said Brian's ghost as he twerked away.

The following day was a faerie folk holiday recognized by the Special Unit called Queensday. Queensday is a touchy subject at Collins House, as it celebrates the famous Leprechaun Queen called Moira with the World's Most Interesting Forehead. Queen Moira herself was one foot, two inches tall, and her forehead was famous for being not all that interesting. She had a firm stance that the wee folk should make all humans into sausages and annex Ireland as a suburb of Tir Na Nog. Obviously, this is a hot-button issue, as Queen Moira's politics are not very popular with the human crowd, but she is a superstar in leprechaun history. At some point, everyone decided to let the wee folk have their day to celebrate her and not make a thing out of it. Either way, the Special Unit has the day off.

I took the train into Cork and then changed on to Dublin to visit my folks at the Joy. I brought Mum and Da falafel sandwiches from the Cafe Oasis, not too far from the prison, and after they were smashed, inspected, taken apart, and then put back together at the security checkpoint, we sat and ate them, catching up.*

I showed off my new uniform to Mum and Da, twirling an imaginary shillelagh, since mine was being held at the guard's desk.

---

* Falafels still taste great after being smashed up, as they are made from chickpeas that have already been smashed up. There's really nothing you can do to falafel that hasn't already been done to it.

I told my folks of my recruitment to the Special Unit, and they *ooh*ed and *hmmmm*ed with great interest.

"The Garda of Tir Na Nog! Brilliant! Who ever knew of such a thing?" said Mum.

"I always thought the wee folk were made up. The folks that put candy in your shoes?" said Da.

"I used to think that, too." I nodded. "But far from it. I'm not some Galway Garda intern anymore. Maybe my position could even help me find the Bog Man."

"Oh, bless you, Ronan. You look like a superhero!" said Mum, squeezing me.

"You think, Fiona?" asked Da, his eyes locked on the complimentary socks that never stay up. "I mean . . . of course he does, such a strapping lad. And the beret almost works!"

Nobody who's ever met me would call me "strapping," but compared to my da, I actually am. And there's nothing he or anybody could say to make me doubt the beret. I love it.

We sat at a metal table under the lights that make everyone look seasick, and I told them about the remarkable last twelve weeks of my life. About Collins House and how it's sometimes a picnic table. About my classes and about Log, Dermot, and Tim the Medium-Sized Bear, while their eyes cycled through various phases of shock and disbelief.

"He sounds like a pretty big bear," said Da.

"No, trust me," I said. "He's very much medium-sized."

When we had finished our falafels, I laid out my progress in their legal troubles.

"Good news—I've written to the judge, who has assured me that the case will not be reopened unless there is a major new piece of evidence," I told them with excitement.

"But that's terrible news, Ronan," said Mum.

"I don't think we're likely to find much new evidence," added Da.

"Oh, I think we will—or rather, I will," I said with a sly smile. "Because I've got a plan. A plan that goes in motion this very night."

"Oh, bless you!" said Mum, tears welling up in her eyes. "I'd tell you to be careful and not to meddle in all of this, but honestly, two years here in the Joy has taken a real toll on your father and me. We need to tell him, Brendan."

Their faces got quite serious as they took each other's hands.

"We didn't know when to tell you this, so I'll just say it: Your mother and I have had to join two different gangs," said Da.

"It's just for protection purposes, but I'm in the Hutch Gang, and your father is in the Kinahans," said Mum.

"Mum and I are fine—in fact, as much in love as ever. But the gangs are mortal enemies. Kinahans run the prison with an iron fist. We take no guff, especially from the dimwit planks in the Hutch Gang," said Da.

"Actually, Ronan, Hutch Gang is number one. Kinahans are a bunch of cabbages who better watch their mouths, or else," said my mum, a former museum curator and one of the most polite people I've ever met, pulling her finger across her neck in a threatening manner.

"Again, it's mostly for protection, Ronan," said Da.

"But there's a social aspect. The camaraderie and all. And I'd be lying if I didn't say there was a wee bit of fun, knowing I'm in the top gang in the Joy," giggled Mum.

"Now, now, Fiona. Hutch Gang is a bunch of knobs who

are gonna get their clocks cleaned if they don't mind their step," said Da, forming his fingers into a letter *K*, which was clearly the gang sign for the Kinahan Gang.

"Mum, Da, this is horrible! You're the people who do the crossword puzzle in ink. You're the people who taught me how to apologize in French and five different fun ways to fold napkins! You're museum people, not prison gang people!" I said, shaking my head in disbelief.

"Shhh," said Mum, nodding to a guard nearby. "The walls have ears. And it's not like we've gotten the tattoos yet, Ronan."

"Although there has been pressure, and the Kinahans have a pretty smart-looking tattoo, wouldn't look too bad on the ol' biceps," said Da to himself, flexing what he must have thought was his biceps muscle.

"Tattoos?! No, I forbid it," I said firmly, "and I want you to go and quit those gangs today."

"Well, it's not that simple, Ronan," said Mum. "Hutch Gang means Hutch Gang for life."

"And Kinahans is to the grave," added Da. "To. The. Grave."

"Plus, not to brag, but I'm the only woman with a PhD in the whole Hutch Gang!" bragged Mum.

"Stop! That's quite enough. No more gang stuff, you two!" I said.

The guard tapped me on the shoulder, telling me visiting time was up. I was certainly concerned about what my parents had just told me, but I also knew in my heart that they were lovely, well-read people who would be a solid addition to any prison gang.

"There'll be new evidence soon, I promise. Perhaps by tonight!" I said.

As I was buzzed through the visitors' gate, I called over my shoulder with one last warning. "No tattoos, please!"

I changed into my civilian clothes in the Mountjoy visitors' loo, putting my cadet uniform and shillelagh into a duffel bag. I took a right out the prison gate and cut down through pretty Blessington Street Park.

Lord Desmond Dooley's gallery is in a creepy old building at number 12 Henrietta Street, which is a creepy old street. It had started to thunderstorm by the time I arrived, but I had an umbrella, as I was now a devotee of Yogi Hansra and ready for surprises. I mentally prepared for my impromptu little mission in the Spar Grocery on Bolton Street. Out the window I could keep an eye on Dooley's gallery—while pretending to read the label on a can of Batchelor's Mushy Peas for about twenty minutes. Soon the store manager was giving me an annoyed, sidelong glance.*

I felt like I had suddenly caught the stomach flu. My face felt hot to the touch of my hand. I had never actually met Lord Desmond Dooley before. Would he recognize me from the trial? Perhaps confronting him was not a good idea at all. But I had a plan. To be safe, I pulled my hoodie up and tucked my glasses into my pocket. I set down the peas, which smacked to the floor, as without my glasses I have very little depth perception and missed the shelf by several inches. I took a deep breath and left the Spar, clicking my umbrella up against the downpour.

---

* The ingredients of Batchelor's Mushy Peas are: "peas (89%), water, sugar, salt, colour." You can read them in approximately two seconds.

A disconcertingly loud digital doorbell chimed as I entered Dooley's gallery, shaking off my umbrella. The bell was the only modern touch in this spooky place. The gallery is a dank crypt, with the oddly pleasant mold smell of old churches. Stained-glass windows featuring random saints were hung up for sale, with small but steep prices on dangling tags. There were racks with dozens of swords, a few thousand copper bowls, and a variety of pikes, cudgels, and frightening head-smacking devices of the Iron and Bronze Ages. I took a closer look at a pair of ancient leather flip-flops, which were labeled as having belonged to a Saint Colmán of Cloyne, whoever that was. The label read "600"—although I'm not sure if this was the price or the date.

The face of the man behind the desk was obscured by a copy of Oscar Wilde's *The Happy Prince and Other Tales*, but the withered hand holding the book had the gargoyle quality of the man himself: Lord Desmond Dooley.

Dooley lowered the book, revealing a face that is more like famous cinema vampire Nosferatu than any actual person you have ever seen.

I did my best not to gasp. If Dooley recognized me, his face did not betray it at all. He only performed the slowest blink I have ever seen. Dooley moves unhurriedly, like a reptile saving its body heat—because he basically is.

"This isn't a souvenir shop," hissed Dooley as he scanned me up and down. "If you're looking for knick-knacks or football shirts, there's a Carrolls on Mary Street."

"Oh, no, sir," I stammered. "You're the famous Lord Desmond Dooley, and I—well, my employer, that is—is in the market for very old Irish things. Hard-to-come-by things, if you get my gist?"

I thought it seemed unlikely that a teenager would be in the market for stolen treasures and that me working for a fictional "collector" would be more plausible. Now to get Dooley to slip up and admit that he had stolen the Bog Man.

Dooley's lizard hand pulled a pince-nez off his nose. He thought for a long moment; then something resembling a smile formed at the corners of his mouth.

"And who, exactly, may I ask, is your employer?" he asked.

"A collector who . . . prefers to remain anonymous," I bluffed, as I had not thought this far ahead and my caper was starting to feel underplanned. "But I'm certain he would meet your price for any serious artifacts. Very old things. Perhaps even the oldest available things."

"Yes. Serious artifacts. Your employer and I share the same taste, boy. Nothing but the best. A moment, please."

He ducked behind a purple velvet curtain into a chamber in the back. There was a muted rustling, a clatter, and the sound of something unlocking. A moment later, Dooley's claw-finger curled out and waved me back.

"Come, come, lad—I've got a little something here that you won't see anywhere else."

My stomach did a little hula. The heat from my flushed face was rising, as if I were peering into a pizza oven to see if the pizza was done. I followed Dooley behind the purple curtain, which was disgustingly damp to the touch.

Water dripped, creating a little echo. In the blackness, it was impossible to tell the size of the room, but it sounded vast indeed. Only Dooley's reptile eyes and part of his hand were visible in the flicker of the lamp he held. His hand trembled, and I felt a slight wave of sympathy for the creepy old man.

He beckoned me deeper into the darkness. I could just make out the shadows of what seemed to be large birdcages. Most seemed empty, their bottoms lined with chewed-up pages of the *Irish Times* and large bird droppings. Farther off in the dark, I could hear what sounded like the flutter of wings. Large wings.

"Come closer, lad . . . closer now . . . Ronan Boyle," whispered Dooley as he grabbed me by the hand. My heart stopped. I felt a zap run through my spine as if someone had stepped on my grave in the future.

Clearly, Lord Desmond Dooley knew perfectly well who I was. My under-thought plan was precisely that, and he was now going to do something horrid like chop me up with an ax from the Bronze Age and put me into any number of museum-quality bowls.

"I was wondering when you might pay me a visit, Cadet."

Without warning, Dame Judi Dench leaned in to me

and said, "Hold my gummy worms, Ronan Boyle—I'm off to the loo." This is because I had once again gone to my imaginary safe place, and Dame Judi was just ducking out to the loo, which left me defenseless and alone, holding fictional gummy worms. I smacked into reality as Dooley's hand perched on my shoulder like an Indonesian bat's feet—hard, his nails taking purchase in the fabric of my hoodie.

He pulled me toward a stack of old stones arranged like a table, or the kind of Stonehenge-type things you would see out in the Burren. It gave the room the feeling that perhaps this was the altar of some sinister church. My instinct was to flee back to the Spar Grocery, but Dooley's grip on my shoulder prevented this.

"Who? What's this now? I certainly don't know what you're talking about. Ronan who?" I stammered, playing dumb, which was not all that far from the truth. "I'll just go and tell my grown-up employer . . . But he'll be expecting me, and he gets very cross, so I had better run along right away!"

"Now listen up, Cadet Ronan Boyle," hissed Dooley into my ear with breath that was surprisingly cold and

unsurprisingly rancid. His nails now pinched through my hoodie and into the meat part of my shoulder. I winced. "You've come looking for the Bog Man. And why wouldn't you, with your poor mum and da in the Joy after the scandal? I admire your bravery. As for your folks—they never saw it coming. In some ways, I feel sorry for them. But somebody had to take the fall, you see. It's not my decision. All of this rawmaish. There are larger forces at work than Lord Desmond Dooley, lad. And If you don't fear me, that's fine. But even I fear the others."

At this point Dame Judi was back from the loo in the movie theater that exists in my mind. "Buck up, Ronan Boyle—show some spine, you #$@&%! Say something!" said the imaginary Dame, using a filthy expletive that I will not write down, as it's unbecoming of our generation's finest actress and a Dame Commander of the Order of the British Empire. She yanked the gummy worms from my hand and bonked me across the face with the box. Because even fictional Dame Judi Dench has no problem saying what she feels.

"I'm on to you, mate. And you'll pay if it's the last thing you do!" I blurted into Dooley's face.

Dooley stumbled, startled, losing his grip on my shoulder. I also fell backward. I was as startled as he was.

Dooley's dead eyes lit up. He seemed to laugh, but no sound came out of him.

"Good on you, Boyle. If our places were flipped, I'd take the stuffing out of you, too. But I assure you, you won't find the Bog Man around here, because I don't have him. And contrary to what you've heard, I did not sell him. You have any idea what a four-thousand-year-old Irish mummy is worth, Boyle?"

". . . Not really?" I said.

"LESS THAN YOU WOULD THINK!" howled Dooley, shaking his clenched little claws in frustration. He lurched toward me, trying to loom over me, even though I am a good deal taller than him. He picked a moldy box up off the stone slab, about the size of a child's coffin, because it was, in fact, a child's coffin.

"But don't let my pity turn to anger. If I ever see you poking around again, you'll get a surprise like this one."

He put the coffin in my hands. The lid burst open.

The next moment was a blur in its brevity and violence. A wee woman with bright red eyes and a nose that looked like it was accidentally put on upside down leaped out of the coffin. She was truly hideous, with the underbite of a shih tzu. She stood less than sixteen inches tall. She was musking hard, clearly riled up, and the smell of old fish heads blasted from her every pore. She poked both my eyes with her brass shillelagh and bit me squarely on the nose. I tumbled backward, and she pounced onto my chest. Most of her body weight seemed to actually be contained in her dense, gold shoes. She gave a kick to my chin, causing me to bite down on my tongue. She made a gesture so rude and insulting that I had to look it up later in the library at Collins House. She blew her nose at me, misting my face with a light drizzle of leprechaun snot. She then turned about, pointed her bum at me, and delivered a brief but angry toot—as if to add a nasty exclamation point to this whole mess.

My tongue hurt too much to scream, so I made a Frankenstein sound. I could taste the blood in my mouth. Obviously, nothing quite like this had ever happened to me before. I have no specific recollection of how, exactly, I got out of Dooley's gallery, but I must have bolted right quick. The next thing that I remember I was standing in the Spar Grocery again, sticking my poor nose and tongue into a freezer filled with Cadbury Flake Twinpot desserts and missing my umbrella.

An hour or so later, I was on the train from Heuston Station, still trembling and holding my nose, which now displayed several small teeth marks. I ate six of the frozen Cadbury Flakes that the annoyed Spar store manager had insisted I purchase after touching them with my cut nose and tongue. They were wonderful and greatly helped to settle my distressed body and mind.

I'm certain that Lord Desmond Dooley meant to frighten me away forever. But deep down I knew that the next time I crossed paths with him . . .

I would be more prepared.

Also, I would get my umbrella back at some point, as it is a nice umbrella.

CHAPTER SIX

THE MALTON HOTEL ROBBERY

I t was late in the day when I arrived back at the barracks, and it took me several tries to nail the song that reveals Collins House. My tongue was throbbing, and the tricky middle part eluded me. I lugged myself up the spiral stairs and related the day's strange events to Log. This was the first time in ages that she did not chuckle under her breath. Seeing that I was deeply distressed, Log sang me a song in the language of the animals, which was lovely, even though I did not understand the words.

I am a touch embarrassed to say it, but I fell asleep in Log's huge arms, and it was the deepest I had slept in months. When I awoke, she was giggling softly in her sleep, in her usual deranged manner. But at this point I had come to find it comforting.

At dusk, when I was getting into my cadet uniform, the intercom in the barracks buzzed.

"Boyle! Report to Captain de Valera at the porte cochere,"* whinnied Jeanette O'Brien's voice, in what sounded like her horse manifestation.

I adjusted the optional cadet beret that I love and hustled to the porte cochere, which was an eight-minute run to the opposite end of the house.

When I arrived, dripping sweat, Captain de Valera was scratching the neck of a rust-colored Irish wolfhound so large that, on first sight, I thought it was a pony.

"This is Lily," said the captain, nodding to the wolfhound. "Lily, this is new cadet Ronan Boyle. Say hello."

---

* *Porte cochere* is just a fancy word for covered driveway.

I waited for the dog to say something and then realized that Captain de Valera intended for me to say hello to the dog.

"She doesn't talk. She's a dog, of course," said the captain.

"Oh, right," I stammered. "Nice to meet you, Lily. I'm Ronan Boyle." I put out my hand, and the hound put her massive paw in it, almost pulling me to the ground.

"Now, to the Malton Hotel—on the double, Boyle. There's been a robbery," she said as she tossed me a set of keys. I stared at them dumbfounded—one of my best skills.

"But I don't drive, Captain," I protested. "Never have. Haven't got a license. Can't even get one for a year, even if I wanted to."

"Then you'd better not get pulled over," she quipped as she hopped into the back of the jeep. "Pat Finch has been my driver for years. But I'm afraid his latest psychological evaluation by the Special Unit deemed him Class One: T.A.T.D.—Too Angry to Drive—even in Ireland. Can you imagine, Boyle?"

"Finch? Too angry? Yes, I can."

"You'll never catch me driving on this island, Boyle—I'm not an eejit." She was not kidding. From this point on I would be her new driver, even though this was both technically and not technically illegal.

After several false starts, sputters, stalls, and a brief jaunt in reverse, just eighteen minutes later I was driving the captain's jeep—the camouflaged one with the mysterious plates that I had seen out at Clifden Castle. It turns out that the harp on the license plate is the classification of Special Unit vehicles; the number is always seven, just because it's lucky and because Irish people are superstitious.

My fingers were gripped on the wheel so hard that they cramped up, and it was a bit of an effort to remove them later. I did my best to keep the vehicle to the far left of the road, running into the ditch a few times and keeping well below the speed limit. The captain was engrossed in a report and seemed not to notice or care that I was doing a rubbish job of driving her.

Captain de Valera was in the backseat with her high leather boots up, and Lily was in the passenger seat to my left. This would become our standard seating arrangement. To this day, I have never really known why Captain Siobhán de Valera picked me to be her protégé. The closest I have come to understanding was when I once overhead her telling another officer that I had a "nice-seeming face, yet is not so bright as to get fancy and insubordinate."

When we arrived at the charming Malton Hotel in Killarney, two local garda led the captain, Lily, and myself into the office, where the manager, one Mr. Doherty—a sweaty, redheaded man of about fifty—was nearly in tears.

"All of it gone, every last drop!" he whimpered into a handkerchief that was wiping either sweat or tears from his face.

"Start at the beginning," said Captain de Valera.

"Come, see for yourself," said Mr. Doherty, and we all fell in behind him as he opened a hidden panel in a bookcase, revealing a passage that descended into the depths of the hotel.

When we arrived at the bottom, I saw that it was the most magnificent wine cellar you're likely to find in this part of the country. The racks were made from varnished cherry, and the most exquisite detail had gone into carving the wood. The shelves were divided by wine region: Rhônes, Burgundies, Loire Valley, etc. The most notable detail about this shrine was the complete and total absence of even a single bottle of wine.

"We've been looted!" said Mr. Doherty, his voice trembling. "Probably thirty thousand euros' worth of wine. And nobody heard a thing. That's why we suspected that perhaps the wee folk were involved."

"No one move, please," said the captain as she raised her shillelagh to make sure no one trampled across the floor. "Lily, work."

Lily did a quick trot around the perimeter of the room, letting her nose hover for a moment in a few specific spots. A dog's sense of smell is a thousand times stronger than a human's and can pick up minute traces of the past. She returned to the captain and thumped a massive paw twice, wobbling her head to the right and growling in a low rumble.

"What's she saying?" asked Mr. Doherty.

"She doesn't talk," replied the captain. "She's a dog. But she smells the cologne of a gancanagh."

Lily thumped again, firmly. This time accompanied by two short barks. "Leprechaun musk, too," added the captain. "Mr. Boyle, would you be so kind as to check for prints?"

I clicked on my torch and lowered down next to Lily, checking for shoe marks. I crawled for several moments, but all I could find were three sets of large human shoes and one partial leprechaun shoe print. The leprechaun's print was Triskelion, a faerie pattern featuring three legs running, like a wheel.*

The captain nodded, pleased.

"Something tiny has climbed these wine racks," I continued as my torch illuminated a filthy handprint on the wood. "Someone really small, judging by the distance

---

* Identifying leprechaun shoe-print patterns is the most tedious part of Practices of Irish and Faerie Law.

between marks, and he seems to be missing one finger on his left hand."

"A tiny climber with nine fingers. A fortune in French wines. The smell of the cologne of a gancanagh and leprechaun musk," said the captain as she paced, pensively twirling her oak-root shillelagh, as was her custom. "A man would be a fool in these parts to keep thirty thousand euros' worth of wine behind a secret door that has not been faerie-proofed. Mr. Doherty, you're aware that the Special Unit provides faerie-proofing for a mere fifteen euros a year?"

Mr. Doherty's face fell with embarrassment. Clearly, he knew the captain was right. Leprechauns, trolls, far darrigs, merrows—almost all of the faerie folk of Ireland love to have a drink and make merry. They love to sip wine, port, whiskey, rum, or stout as much as they love to smoke pipes, swap babies for wood, play tricks on unicorns, hide gold, and bewitch human kitchen appliances.

Leaving a treasure trove of excellent wine in a place where the wee folk could access it would cost Mr. Doherty and the hotel a three-hundred-euro fine—this is standard practice of the Special Unit, to encourage humans to keep their wines and spirits out of faerie sight, out of faerie mind. (There is a poster in the Supply and Weapons Department at Collins House with this exact phrase on it.)

"Mr. Boyle, write up a warning for Mr. Doherty, please," said the captain, being very generous as she tossed me a black leather ledger.

"Indeed, it sounds like the work of a team. If it is in fact a gancanagh and a nine-fingered leprechaun working together, I wouldn't be surprised if it's Lovely Liam and Wee Glen with the Gorgeous Ears," said the captain, clicking her shillelagh onto the hooks on her back with a deftness that I truly envied.

"Lovely Liam, per his record, is a known and registered gancanagh," said the captain. "Gancanaghs are almost human-sized. They can't shape-shift, but they can seem to vanish into thin air."

"How?" I asked.

"With the amazing ability to blend into their surroundings," said the captain. "Like a chameleon. They pick up the colors and patterns of things around them. But mind yourself, Boyle, the biggest thing to fear about gancanaghs—when they're not hiding, they're off-the-charts beautiful."

"Wait, what?" I said, ever so eejitlike.

"Aye. Gancanaghs are so extremely gorgeous, in fact, that most humans who see one will fall instantly in love," said the captain. "This would be funny, if gancanaghs weren't also faerie folk, whose very raison d'être is to trick and steal from humans. Fall in love with a gancanagh, and the next thing you know you've just given them your entire flock of sheep or perhaps all of your clothes or your very finest buggy. I once handled a case of a human in Athlone who fell so fast for a gancanagh that he gave her three gold teeth from his own mouth before she vanished right before his eyes at a kebab and pizza takeaway restaurant. She also stole his kebab. This is the level of mischief you're talking about with gancanaghs."

I had now learned more in the field with Captain de Valera than I had during twelve weeks of Wise Young Jim's Practices of Irish and Faerie Law class.

"Wee Glen with the Gorgeous Ears is a wanted leprechaun with a lazy eye and a rap sheet twice as long as his stinky beard. He lost a finger in a dustup with a bloodthirsty unicorn named Tom McNamara.* Currently he's wanted on an open case in Kerry for bewitching the butter churn of a Mrs. Eileen Murphy. Of course, Mrs. Murphy was a fool indeed for accepting the 'gift' of a butter churn that makes endless butter. Wee Glen gave it to the woman instead of his crock of gold. But there was no way to *stop* the butter churn. Three days later, Mrs. Murphy was nearly drowned in eight feet of pure Irish butter in her sitting room. I was there when emergency workers cut a hole in the thatched roof and pulled her out. She was barely alive, but she also had the most beautiful skin of her entire life. In fact, she looked five years younger than before she went into the butter. This is the power of Irish butter, Boyle."

I ripped the warning slip out of the ledger and handed

---

* Unicorns aren't as precious with their names as leprechauns.

it to Mr. Doherty, who nodded thanks, knowing he'd just barely skirted a three-hundred-euro fine.

"Come, Boyle," said the captain. "Lovely Liam and Wee Glen will have fled to Tir Na Nog by now. Now, what's the closest geata?" Captain de Valera said to herself as she pulled out a small leather book and unlocked the cover with two different keys—one from a chain around her neck and another one from around her wrist.

She began searching through the pages. As Wise Young Jim had told us before nodding off during our first class, this book is one of the most classified documents of the Special Unit. It's a map, divided by county, of all of the aos sí geataí in Ireland.

"Geataí" is the Irish word for *gates*, and "aos sí" is the old-fashioned word for *faerie*. The book has the location of the passageways to and from Tir Na Nog. The one thing to know about the gates is that they never look like something you would expect. Many people talk about the faerie mounds in the north and the strange monoliths out in the Burren, but the faeries have left these in plain sight to draw our attention away from the actual gates. Obviously humans will notice things that look like Stonehenge or mysterious slabs with Celtic symbols—but we're not likely to bother with an old barrel of stagnant water or a pile of horse manure (in an area suspiciously devoid of horses).

The geataí are designed to keep humans away, either with intense boredom or profound fear. And fear would be the protector of the first geata that I would pass through with Captain de Valera and Lily, just fifteen minutes later. And while it was the first of many I've been through at this point in my career, I'll never forget how frightened I was.

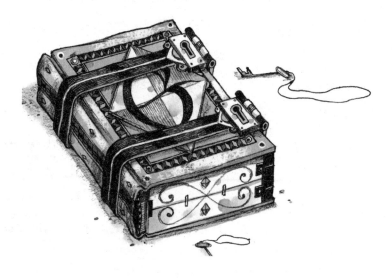

POLITE WARNING!

The next few pages contain the graphic details of a disgusting incident in Castleisland. More sensitive readers may wish to continue Mr. Boyle's journals eight pages from this point.

Your "friend,"

Finbar Dowd
Deputy Commissioner
Special Unit of Tir Na Nog

CHAPTER SEVEN

TIR NA NOG

It was past midnight when we arrived at the closest geata, due north on the N22 in the little town of Castleisland.

Castleisland isn't really an island. And the castle fell down and lies in ruins. But if you had been in Castleisland nine hundred years ago, you would have been blown away by the humongous castle that looked just like an island, with the River Maine diverted into a moat around it. You would have wanted to take a picture of the magnificent fortress with your phone, but you would not have one, because it is nine hundred years ago.

The specific location of the geata is no longer classified, as it was accidentally destroyed a few months later. So, I can tell you that this particular gate was an old refrigerator in the alley behind the Yang Yang Chinese restaurant. Taped to the door was a handwritten note that read WORKS! PLEASE TAKE ME! FREE! Clearly this note was the sinister work of faerie folk, guaranteeing that no human would have touched it for decades.

What I was not expecting when the captain opened the refrigerator door was that on the inside of it would be the ugliest fear gorta I have ever seen. It took me a moment to realize that I was the one who was screaming in such a high-pitched frenzy.

I had never seen a fear gorta in person before and have seen very few since. A fear gorta is a sinewy, not-quite-dead goblin—as gaunt as a human skeleton, with bones nearly popping through its translucent gray skin and eyes bulging from their sockets. While fear gortas look frightening, the more you know about them, the more frightened you should be. Fear gortas date back to the great potato famine and are sometimes called hunger-men. They will eat literally anything.

"People?" you ask. "Do they eat people, Ronan Boyle?"

"Oh yes, they eat people," I reply to your hypothetical question. Because fear gortas love eating humans even more than they love drinking ginger beer. (Apparently, humans taste amazing with ginger beer.)

This particular fear gorta had been asleep when Captain de Valera opened the door and surprised him. He was as unhappy to see us as we were to see him. He let out a howl that vibrated into my bones. His slack jaw hung wide open, revealing a mouth full of rotten fangs that would make even the bravest dentist gag.

Without missing a beat, Captain de Valera gave several deft swings with her shillelagh, landing hard hits to the fear gorta's body and face.

The fear gorta moaned, burped out some flies, and

lurched toward us. With both hands, I unholstered my shillelagh and took a huge swing. I whacked the side of the fear gorta's head with a hard swat. With a wet crack, the creature's head popped off and flew down the alley, only coming to a stop when it hit the back door of the Yang Yang Chinese restaurant. Twelve weeks of being thwacked, poked, and bonked by Yogi Hansra had paid off in my shillelagh skills.

Being apart from its head did not slow down the fear gorta as much as it might have you or me. The fear gorta's body went stumbling around blindly, searching for its noggin. The head grunted, trying to call its body to it like the most disgusting game of Marco Polo you would ever want to see.

Lily the wolfhound was much faster than the fear gorta's aimless, headless body. She picked up the severed head in her mouth, ran to a nearby patch of dirt, and quickly buried it, thumping the earth down hard atop it with her massive paws. It was done with such efficiency that it was clearly not the first time Lily had buried a moaning, not-quite-dead head. Lily trotted back to Captain de Valera, who patted the dog and gave her a white Tic Tac to rid her mouth of the foul aftertaste of fear gorta head.

"You okay, Boyle?" she asked. "You can breathe now. Once you bury the head, a fear gorta goes from nearly dead to all the way dead."

I nodded that I was okay, even though this was a slight exaggeration. To settle my rattled nerves, I found myself stroking Lily's head, which would become something I would do quite a bit over the next several years, to calm myself in stressful situations. Lily, who was more accustomed to life-or-death scenarios than me, nuzzled her head into my hand, seeming to understand and wanting to help me feel calm. To this day, Lily the wolfhound has been one of the best partners I've ever had in the Special Unit. I was proud to be the human who would later give her the Medal of Valor when she had risen to the rank of Major Canine. I should also note that Lily weighs 180 pounds. That's thirty pounds more than me, so when Lily decides to protect you, it's a nice feeling, as there are many creatures—

including some unicorns and sheeries—that run from the sight of Lily.

"We'll be passing through the geata now and into the land of faerie folk. There, we have to observe their laws," said the captain, using the confusing homophones of *there* and *their*.

"The good news is, there are almost no laws in Tir Na Nog, so use your wits and try not to get eaten by anything," she added, pulling her leather gloves to tighten them up. "And never, ever accept gold from a leprechaun, for it always comes with a curse."

"Check," I said, trying to sound brave.

"Watch your step, shillelagh at the ready, and when in doubt, just stay behind me," she said. "Ready? Off we go, lad."

I'm not sure if I actually said yes or just nodded my head. But I can tell you that I certainly was not really ready.

Captain de Valera took me by the shoulders, as if she were about to lead me in a dance. Then she pulled me backward into the refrigerator.

The best way I can describe the feeling of passing through a geata is that it's like when you are coming down a flight of stairs and you misjudge the number of steps by a factor of one, and your body lurches and you flap your arms like the wings of a terrified penguin who has been thrown aloft by some cruel person who hates penguins.

One second later, we were on the other side. We had crashed down into broad daylight and the most gorgeous honey-colored woodland stream you have ever seen. Lily landed a moment after us, creating a huge splash with her massive body. I suddenly became aware of just how different Tir Na Nog is, for the stream seemed to be made of pure whiskey.

"Is that what I think it is?" I asked the captain, sniffing.

"Indeed," whispered Captain de Valera. "Single malt whiskey. I wouldn't dare drink it if I were you." She gestured to a nearby unicorn that was lapping at the whiskey river. He was a large male, sixteen hands high, with a deep blue coat and an onyx dowser. The unicorn turned, stumbled, and walked drunkenly into a tree, lodging his sharp dowser deep into the trunk.

"Ninety proof at least—that's very strong stuff. Too strong, in fact," said the captain.

The blue unicorn wriggled himself free of the tree and staggered off into the woods, singing "The Irish Rover" as terribly as you've ever heard it and getting many of the words wrong.

"Lucky he didn't see us," said the captain. "Unicorns are violent and unpredictable."

I unbuttoned the neck part of my jumpsuit, as the lowlands of Tir Na Nog are a tropical climate—much warmer than the human Republic of Ireland. I was starting to sweat. My heart was racing.

For reference, here is a basic map of Tir Na Nog, land of the faerie folk, drawn by your friend Ronan Boyle.

The Floating Lakes shown here are not to scale. In reality, they contain several hundred smaller lakes, rivers, and tributaries. And the snow-covered mountains to the north are hypothetical, as no human garda officer has ever seen them as of the time that I am writing this. The volcano is as accurate as I can draw it, and there are far more towns than are shown here.

TIR·NA·NOG

SHENANOGRAM

Captain de Valera pulled a bronze compass from her belt and began making some adjustments to tiny dials on it. This device is carried by many in the Special Unit and is called a shenanogram, as it points toward where shenanigans are happening, and where you find shenanigans, you'll find the wee folk.

"Looks like we're about two kilometers from Nogbottom," said the captain. "It's the second-largest town of the leprechauns and the last known residence of Wee Glen with the Gorgeous Ears. Come, Lily. Come, Boyle."

And off the three of us went into the foreboding Forest of Adair, with the sound of giant cow-sized toads bellowing somewhere in the foliage ahead of us.

The Forest of Adair is named after an old leprechaun king named Adair with the Oh-So-Lovely Feet, who held the weddings to all of his thirty-nine wives in the forest. All of the wives left King Adair, usually fleeing the marriage union after just a few weeks. Records show that his feet were not that lovely at all, he was incredibly boring, and he had the strange ability to snore out of his bottom while he slept.

The forest itself is technically a subtropical rain forest and contains several thousand varieties of plant species that are unique to Tir Na Nog, such as currywood trees—which smell exactly like very good massaman curry and can grow to be three hundred meters tall. Another specimen of the forest is the omnivorous plant called the Kissing Colleen. The Kissing Colleen is probably the worst-named plant in Tir Na Nog. Clurichauns named the plant as an ironic joke. (Clurichauns are not funny at all.) While the Kissing Colleen smells lovely and looks like a large purple gardenia that's bending over to "kiss" you, it also has a three-foot tongue that's as fast as a lizard's and five rows of razor-sharp teeth. A healthy adult Kissing Colleen plant can eat three leprechauns a week, and they will even eat a unicorn foal—although it takes them many days to digest such a large creature.

Lily the wolfhound led the way through the forest, sniffing and occasionally marking certain spots with her scent. Captain de Valera pulled a small piece of chalk from her belt and drew arrows on some of the currywood trees, pointing back the way we had come.

"Sometimes, the trick's not getting into Tir Na Nog, Boyle," she said, "but rather remembering how to get out."

The ground in the Forest of Adair is made of soft, spongelike peat—which is five thousand years of decomposed plant material packed into a lovely mush. It's a delight to walk upon. But in certain spots one must watch out for fastpeat. Fastpeat looks exactly like normal peat, so there's no way to watch out for it, which is what I just told you to do. Apologies for that. The only way to know you've stepped in fastpeat is that you've just sunk deep into the ground and will likely soon die from drowning.

Luckily for me, one moment later as I sank to my chest into the peat and yelped like a confused billy goat, Captain de Valera caught me by linking her shillelagh with mine.

"Precisely why I said to keep your shillelagh ready," said the captain as she pulled me out. Lily grabbed hold of my jumpsuit in her teeth and helped her yank me up.

I caught my breath and vowed that I would be more careful. But since there's no way to look out for fastpeat, there was no way I could keep this vow. As it turned out, I

would fall into fastpeat two more times—Captain de Valera would fall one time, and Lily one time, too—before we finally arrived at the bluffs.

The bluffs loom over a chasm, several hundred feet straight down. The bottom of the canyon far below looked like a river, but on closer inspection it was actually a vast swath of four-leaf clovers undulating in the wind—so much bright green clover that it created the illusion of water, rippling with a current. Across the chasm, in the sky, was a tornado of hundreds of rainbows twisting and swirling together. Even in Tir Na Nog rainbows always point toward leprechauns and their pots of gold, so when you have an entire city full of leprechauns, it's bound to have a violent rainbow storm swirling above it.

"Nogbottom," said the captain, pointing to the multi-colored typhoon. "We'll have to cross that bridge to get to the town itself." And her finger drew a line from the town to the ruins of what looked like an ancient stone aqueduct.

"But . . . how?" I asked, as the bridge was clearly broken in the middle, providing no pathway to the other side of the chasm.

"It's the Bridge of Riddles, guarded by a far darrig whose name we have never guessed," said the captain. "If we can answer one of his riddles, the bridge will be complete for a moment. Then we run for it."

A moment later, Lily, the captain, and I arrived at the keeper's house below the Bridge of Riddles. Sure enough, a far darrig whose name nobody has ever guessed was just finishing his lunch, which seemed to be some sort of potato and leek pie with onions, white truffles, and tarragon. It smelled delicious.

"Give us a minute, luvs," said the far darrig as he wiped his rat snout with a napkin. He rose from his comfy chair in the keeper's house and tucked his tail back into his britches. He refastened his belt and put his hat back on, groaning and stretching his tiny little body. Far darrigs tend to look like red wombats, with stubby little tusks that jut up from an underbite that they all seem to share. This one's body was almost a perfect circle, and under his snout his fur was brushed into a mustache. He wrapped the unfinished portion of his amazing-smelling pie in the napkin and waddled toward us. "Three euros fifty for the riddle, please," he said. "Each."

"Do we pay for the dog as well?" I asked as the captain counted some money from yet another pouch on her crowded utility belt.

"No, just for the beefies," said the far darrig, using a derogatory name for humans that many faerie folk use. As the story goes, "beefies" is slang for humans because we smell so much like meat to faerie folk, but the real meaning of the term dates back to the time when Ireland was under British control, and the Queen's Patrolmen of Tir Na Nog were a division of the Yeomen Warders—the guardians of the Tower of London. These Yeoman Warders, even today, are called Beefeaters, and that is the real reason that we humans have this nickname amongst faerie folk.

Captain de Valera handed him ten euros, and he took what seemed like forever to make change, squinting at the coins.

"Let's see, let's see," mumbled the far darrig. "A riddle to keep the beefies out of Nogbottom." He flipped through a giant, dusty tome of riddles with his stubby claws. "Ah, here's a gem," he said as he closed the book and locked it.

This is the riddle the unnamed far darrig gave us, as best I remember it:

> *I always trot, yet make no sound,*
> *when babies come, the da gets round,*
> *and though I'm equine through and through,*
> *you'll find me in the deepest blue.*

The riddle hung there in the air for a moment. I tried to make sense of the words as best I could. *Da* is how Irish people say "dad," so this was a major clue. Sometimes, when I'm in a spot like this, as I often was in primary school, I picture my memories as card catalogs, like those you would find in a library. In my imagination, I opened drawer after drawer, trying to remember an animal where the male carries the baby in its stomach. It was right on the tip of my tongue.

Perhaps not quite on the tip of my tongue, as several moments passed. You may have already figured the riddle out.

When I finally reached the drawer in my mind labeled *S*, it came to me, plain as day. "Seahorse!" I yelped out with delirious joy. "The horse that does not trot, lives in the ocean blue, and the male of the species carries the babies in its belly!"

Captain de Valera shot me a rare smile, knowing that my answer was correct. I wanted to hug her, but I knew that she was my superior officer and that would have been enormously awkward, and so I did not.

"Off you go, then," said the far darrig as he climbed a little ladder and put the weight of his body on a rusted lever, riding it down to the floor and landing with a thud.

There was a massive scraping and groaning as the bridgekeeper's house started to tremble below our feet. Lily barked—directing our attention up to the bridge itself, which was reassembling before our eyes. The stones rolled, slid, and stacked themselves up, like watching a film of its destruction in reverse. In a moment, it was complete.

"Well, that's the strangest thing I've seen today," I said, staring like a buffoon at the bridge and rubbing the sweaty steam off the lenses of my glasses.

"You might want to wait on that decision. The night is young," said Captain de Valera as she ran across the bridge and into Nogbottom.

I took a deep breath. I was about to cross over into Nogbottom, the second-largest city of leprechauns. A city that I would later read about in my training manuals as one of the top five most dangerous places in Tir Na Nog.

Lily barked, calling me along.

And off I went.

Chapter Eight

NOGBOTTOM

I ran along the Bridge of Riddles as fast as my spindly legs could carry me. To my surprise, Lily, the captain, and myself arrived on the other side of it at eight P.M. on Friday night, despite the fact that we had left the bridgekeeper's house on Wednesday in the wee hours of the night.

The time and weather in the land of the faerie folk are deliberately confusing. For example, in Nogbottom, it is always Friday night at eight P.M. The time does not change, ever.

"Why?" you ask. Because that's how the leprechauns like it. Leprechauns love the naughty, carefree feeling that passes over a town on a Friday night at eight P.M., and since there are no clocks or calendars in Tir Na Nog, long ago the wee folk cast a spell over Nogbottom to keep it in a perpetual state that feels like Friday night at eight. In Oifigtown, the capital city of Tir Na Nog and the seat of the leprechaun royal family, it is always a snowy November Monday morning at eleven A.M., as this is the time and type of day that faerie folk will be the most productive.

Being that it was such a warm summer Friday night, the street was bustling with leprechauns riding by on pigs and peacocks with saddles, and even some fancy-dressed tiny men and women riding around on large rabbits. Others, including clurichauns and red men, were tumbling in and out of one of Nogbottom's five hundred pubs. Yes, having only a population of two thousand faerie folk, Nogbottom somehow has five hundred pubs. That's one pub for every four inhabitants. Leprechauns love to sip glasses of stout and porter—but they really go to the pubs to show off their shoes. In Tir Na Nog it's considered rude if you don't put your feet up on the table.

I watched over my shoulder as the Bridge of Riddles crumbled back down into its half-ruined state.

Now we were stranded in this strange town. The street we stood upon was lined on both sides with wooden, leprechaun-sized buildings that appeared to be a thousand years old (they are much older). A tipsy clurichaun rode by me on a pig and shoved me aggressively with his little shoulder.

"Watch yerself, ya daft beefie," he belched at me.

Lily responded to the little man with a bark that blew him right off his pig. "Knocked off me pig" is a popular expression in faerie slang, because it happens so often. Pigs do not like being ridden, and the wee folk drink far too much.

Nogbottom is surrounded by bluffs on all sides, so the residents of the town have had to build their buildings up toward the perpetual rainbow storm in the sky above. The irregular-shaped structures that line the street were stacked up fourteen stories tall. To you or me, this is only

about fifty-six feet, as one floor of a leprechaun building is only four feet high. Little makeshift rope bridges and ladders connected the upper stories to each other like a tiny skyway.

I gazed up and saw many leprechauns darting back and forth between the upper apartments, hanging laundry, gilding their shoes, courting fair leprechaun maidens—the everyday things that the wee folk do. I patted Lily's head. Not to comfort her, but to comfort myself.

Captain de Valera tapped me on the shoulder with her shillelagh and gestured toward a brightly lit theater a few blocks up the street. The venue was named Opera Supreme Magnifico, and it was one of over two dozen theaters in Nogbottom's Left End.

Leprechauns live for thousands of years, and as a result they have developed a very specific theatrical style for their own tastes. Leprechauns love sad musicals—the sadder the better for them. The average leprechaun musical playing in the Left End has a running time of five days—the first act is usually four days, then a huge lunch, then a much shorter second act that is just one day. If you lived to be thousands of years old, five-day musicals would make perfect sense.*

We headed into the bustling Left End, where little carriages zipped by and actors and poets hustled about on their way to their engagements. At little stalls all around, merchants sold trinkets, shoe polish, pipes, and paper baskets full of fried unicorn-and-chips. The greasy smoke

---

* A few years later, I had the privilege of being the guest of my friend Aileen, Whose Luscious Eyes Sparkle Like Ten Thousand Emeralds in the Sun when she opened in a full seven-day performance of *A Bonnet for Bonnie Bobby's Buggy*. To say it was the saddest musical I have ever seen is an understatement. The short version: A widower named Bonnie Bobby weds off his beloved daughter, Clara, to the evil prince of the Bog Lands. She does not love the prince, and so she wishes to never see him again. A sinister clurichaun named Jeff makes her wish come true by permanently attaching a bucket to her head. So, the musical is basically seven full days of a wee woman singing under a bucket about her regrets. At the end, she falls down a well for no apparent reason. Then her father falls down after her. Then her ghost comes back and sings an even sadder song, about how she can't see the afterworld, because the bucket on her head cracked when she fell down the well—making her ghost blind. The only reference to the bonnet for the buggy is that (I think) it's what the evil bog prince gave to Clara's father as a dowry. The only positive thing I can say about *A Bonnet for Bonnie Bobby's Buggy* is that the lunch was fantastic. And the other upside—even after seeing a sad, seven-day musical in Nogbottom, you always get out on Friday at eight P.M., which is before the restaurants get crowded.

made the air thick with its pungent aroma. (Unicorn-and-chips is a popular dish in Nogbottom, because leprechauns love to think that they're eating their natural enemy—the unicorn—but I've seen several reports that one hundred percent of the unicorn meat sold in Nogbottom is actually made from pumpkin filling mixed with chili powder and beets. A leprechaun could no sooner catch a unicorn than you or I could catch an aircraft carrier.)

We stepped carefully through the diminutive crowds so as not to crush anybody. A tiny man in a velvet fourteen-piece suit rode by on a stout female Yorkshire terrier. The captain explained to me that this was a messenger of Raghnall, King of Tir Na Nog, from the capital in Oifigtown. Only the royal family and their messengers are allowed to ride on Yorkshire terriers, the most loyal and attractive dog in either our world or Tir Na Nog.

Lucky for our noses, leprechauns are very comfortable in Nogbottom, so nobody was musking. Although with the food stalls all around and the hideous pipe smoke, I'm not sure I would have even noticed if they were.

Certainly, nobody was happy to see two human garda

officers and a massive wolfhound heading through town, but I should point out: The presence of the Garda Special Unit of Tir Na Nog in the land of faerie folk is entirely legal, and we are protected through three different accords with our respective governments, just the same as the W.G. patrols are protected in the human Republic of Ireland.

(Note: W.G. is an abbreviation of wee gaiscíoch, or "little warriors." THE W.G. ARE THE VERY CORRUPT POLICE FORCE OF THE FAERIE FOLK, COMMONLY CALLED THE WEEGEES. If you are ever stopped and questioned by the weegees—RUN! RUN AS FAST AS YOU CAN. THE WEEGEES, AS OF THE TIME I AM WRITING THIS, HAVE SEVERAL HUMAN PRISONERS IN THEIR PRISON CALLED THE GAOL WHO HAVE NOT BEEN CHARGED WITH A CRIME OR EVEN ALLOWED A PHONE CALL TO THE HUMAN REALM. The weegees have zero regard for the law. For example, in 2001, after a scathing report from Amnesty International, the Special Unit stopped carrying brass shillelaghs, which can cause

fatal injuries. The weegees, and only the weegees, still carry them to this day—no comment.)

As we moved up the cobblestone street, Captain de Valera filled me in on the facts of the case so far.

"The suspect Wee Glen is a recidivist and a registered actor in the Thespians' Guild, which is less of a union, more of a gang," she said, opening her notebook and showing me a mug shot accompanied by the charcoal rubbing of a small, spectacular shoe with the Triskelion pattern. "The pay for theatrical work in Nogbottom isn't what it used to be. Most of the ridiculously inflated ticket prices go to the clurichauns who scalp tickets, so a lot of the wee actors have turned to the quick money in crime and poetry."

Captain de Valera flashed her badge as we ducked into the lobby of the Opera Supreme Magnifico. The ceiling was vaulted and painted with lavish scenes from famous musicals, but it was intended for leprechaun height, so both the captain and I had to crouch as we questioned the strange wee woman who was working in the box office.

Her parents must have been one leprechaun and one

faerie, for she had leprechaun features but also enormous eyes, wings on her shoulders, and hooves where her feet would be. She was chained to the box office desk with an old lead padlock. This was not unusual. If you want faerie folk to do any kind of bookkeeping or accounting work, or basically any work other than mischief, poetry, making shoes, or theatrical acting, you must literally chain them to the desk, as paperwork and tedious things are so against the nature of the wee folk that they will run or fly away.

"Captain de Valera and Cadet Boyle of the Special Unit, ma'am," said the captain to the wee woman.

The wee woman jumped, spilling gold coins in every direction and letting her pipe fall from her mouth onto her desk with a hot splatter of ashes.

"You beefies can't just come in here with your hound and start intimidating me," said the wee woman. "I've got me rights."

Lily was sniffing around the lobby. To the small woman, Lily would look like a grizzly bear.

"We're looking for Wee Glen," said the captain, "wanted for a robbery in Killarney."

"Wee Glen with the Gorgeous Ears or Wee Glen, Whose Voice Is Like a Feather Tickling a Cello on a Summer Afternoon?"

"With the Gorgeous Ears," I chimed in, stretching to my full height and bonking my head on the ceiling like the daft beefie that I am.

"Well, tough luck. I never heard of him," said the wee woman indignantly, finding her pipe and shoving it back into her mouth as if to end the conversation with this gesture.

"You can't have never heard of him. You just told me his name," I said, getting aggressive myself and twirling my hemlock shillelagh as if I were handy with it, which you know I was not yet.

My bluff was more effective than I expected. The little woman squirmed and held up her creepy little webbed fingers in protest.

"I'm not telling you beefies where that devil is. Not

under any circumstances," she said loudly as she picked up a pencil and jotted something down as fast as she could. She passed the paper to the captain and whispered so no one could overhear, her voice trembling, "Wee Glen broke my heart. Left me at the altar in the Forest of Adair in a wedding dress that cost a pretty penny and that I no longer fit into because I have been eating my feelings."

And then the wee woman started to weep. Captain de Valera, who was generally not good with emotional witnesses, patted her solemnly on the wing to comfort her. The wee woman's pipe hung slack from her lip as she sobbed.

"Also, me mum made me special shoes for the day," she sniffled, putting her little fish-scale-covered legs up on the desk to show the most lavish set of tiny horseshoes that had been nailed onto her hooves. They were solid platinum and encrusted with jewels that spelled out LOVE on one hoof and OATH on the other.

It was a pitiful sight indeed. Captain de Valera did her best to comfort the little woman, brushing the strange feathers that made up her bouffant hairstyle.

"I've found a jeweler in Oifigtown who can change them to read LOVE GOATS, or LOVE OAFS, but that's the best he can do. I should go with OAFS, I suppose, since that's my lot in life and I'm frightened of goats," said the wee woman, blowing her nose loudly and disgustingly into her sleeve.

"Thank you for your help, and sorry for your troubles," said the captain as she slipped me the piece of paper that the wee woman had given her.

On it was scribbled the name of a notorious Nogbottom establishment called Bob and Thing's Famous Pickle Parlor. Captain de Valera rolled both her green and her brown eye up simultaneously in disgust.

"The Pickle Parlor is the rock bottom of this town. Nothing but lowlifes. Stay on your toes, Boyle," she said.

Our journey to Bob and Thing's Famous Pickle Parlor took Lily, the captain, and me from the Left End all the way to the far side of Nogbottom, which, it turns out, is about a three-minute walk.

Bob and Thing's Famous Pickle Parlor exists outside of the very few laws of Nogbottom, because it lies below the city limits, as one must ride an ancient hand-crank lift (made from an old pickle barrel) down one of the outer bluffs to the tunnel that leads into the parlor, which is in a cavernous rathskeller below the city.

The captain ordered Lily to wait at the surface as a backup in case we got into serious trouble. Honestly, I didn't always understand the commands between Lily and the captain at this early point in my training, but it seems they knew each other very well, and the one thing that was certain was that Lily could be trusted to the ends of the earth.

As Captain de Valera and I rode down in the lift barrel, we could hear accordion music pumping up from below us. The captain explained to me the history of the place, which goes like this:

Bob and Thing's Famous Pickle Parlor is a speakeasy that was opened in 1723 by a leprechaun named Bob the Giant. (He was two feet, three inches tall.)

His partner was a thing, and nobody ever knew exactly what it was, so they just called him that thing.

Depending on whom you ask, that thing looked either

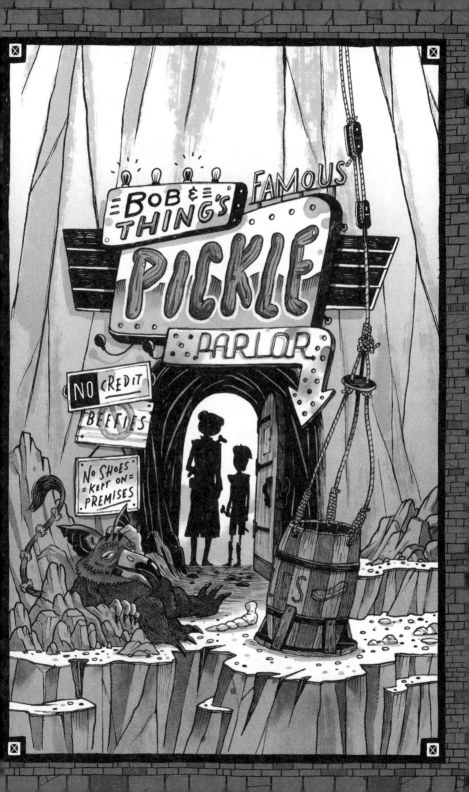

like an enormous bat with tiny wings or a morbidly obese rat with muttonchops—nobody knew much about him, except that he had magnificent back hair that he would brush with a mother-of-pearl comb. That thing was the brains of the operation and famous for his business acumen. Bob was the front man who dealt with customers. Since the day they opened, the Pickle Parlor has served only one thing: pickles, straight out of the barrel.

But not just any pickles. The pickles served at Bob and Thing's Famous Pickle Parlor are one million times spicier than anything a human being could eat.

If a human were to take one bite out of a Pickle Parlor pickle, he would explode. (I regret to say there are memorials in Collins House to two garda officers who attempted to eat the very mildest pickle on the parlor's menu. Their smoldering hats and shoes were found three miles away from Nogbottom in opposite directions.)

But somehow, leprechauns love to eat these pickles. Not just because of the spiciness, but because of the out-of-body experience that comes from eating something that's one million times hotter than a Carolina Reaper.*

So, believe it or not, leprechauns come to Bob and Thing's Famous Pickle Parlor and pay several euros to eat one of these horrible items. What happens next is called the "pickle fits."

Watching leprechauns in the depths of the pickle fits is not a pretty sight. First, the leprechaun turns bright red; then smoke blasts from his ears, nose, and behind. The blast from their bottom is often so powerful that it launches them into the ceiling of the Pickle Parlor (which is padded with old mattresses for this very reason). The next stage of the pickle fits is the unstoppable giggles, and the leprechaun simply cannot stop laughing, while he dances like his insides are full of rattlesnakes and then lets out a burp that often burns off his eyebrows.

And leprechauns love this.

Perhaps the strangest thing of all about the pickle fits is that they only last about twelve seconds, which leads a lot of

---

* A Carolina Reaper is the hottest human pepper that exists, two thousand times hotter than a jalapeño, with a Scoville Heat Unit of over two million.

poor leprechauns to a life of "chasin' the fits," as it's called, where they try to re-create the experience over and over again.

The moldy barrel lift arrived at the entrance to the Famous Pickle Parlor, where a hideous thing (clearly a descendant of the original co-owner) was guarding the door.

This thing's features were batlike, but he had a beak like a toucan, sloth claws, and a thin tail, so even I cannot clarify what category of thing these things are. He had green eyes and fur that glistened like oil. He came up to about my elbow, and in his left claw he twirled a shillelagh made from a unicorn dowser (illegal everywhere since 1951).

This ugly thing blew a wet raspberry at us and tapped an old sign by the door that read NO BEEFIES, NO CREDIT, NO SHOES KEPT ON PREMISES.

The last line of that sign is tragic indeed, for so many of the leprechaun folk love chasin' the fits that they will even trade five-hundred-year-old shoes with twenty-four-carat buckles for a few good "toots at the ceiling."

Without warning, Captain de Valera spun her shillelagh and cracked the hand-claw of the thing, causing him to drop his shillelagh and *ca-caw* in pain from his beak.

This kind of bold attack was Captain Siobhán de Valera's style. She never waited to see how a situation would unfold, but rather she would always make the first move. "Better to be wrong and apologize than be right and do nothing," she would say. She had seen many good Special Unit officers who had hesitated in the wrong situation and been turned into pigs, logs, or waterfalls.

As the ugly, oily thing ducked to grab his shillelagh, the captain delivered a swift knee to his head—her kneecap protector made a satisfying *bonk*, and the thing collapsed. Even though he was out cold, his sentient and seemingly independent tail tried to grab hold of the captain's shille-lagh, but I swatted it out of the air with my staff. (While the standard-issue cadet shillelagh is light, it's also fast and easy to swing, which can be an advantage.)

"Thanks, Boyle," said the captain, collecting herself. "On the other side of that door are the dregs of Nogbottom, scoun-drels who want nothing to do with beefies, let alone garda. Most of 'em are twitching in the pickle fits, so they may pay us no mind. But we may be in for a fight, understand?"

I nodded, wiping sweat from my forehead and

tightening the grip on my shillelagh. I rebuttoned up the top of my jumpsuit again, preparing for the worst.

"If Lovely Liam and Wee Glen are here, and they've got any of the Malton Hotel's wines on them, we can make an arrest. But without any solid proof, we're just working a hunch, and all we can do is question them and let them go about their business."

"Yes, Captain," I said, taking a few warm-up swings.

"And mind you—do not look directly at Lovely Liam under any circumstances. Keep your eyes on his belt or his shoes," she warned. "I can't have you falling in love with a gancanagh on your first day."

"Aye," I said, shaking my head, as I found the idea of me falling in love with a suspect quite silly indeed. I've never even fallen in love—even with my flatmate and terrible guardian Dolores, and she is one of the most beautiful fiddle players in Europe and also a lovely Irish dancer. Plus she makes a potato and crème fraîche soup that will knock your hat off.

The captain held up a glove and counted her fingers down: three . . . two . . .

CHAPTER NINE

THE RAINBOW ROOM

*RUUUNNCH*. Captain de Valera kicked the door off. The hinges exploded with a spark of rust. She lost her balance and fell with the door, managing to ride it like a surfboard. This was not intentional but just a very happy accident. It looked impressive, but she probably couldn't have done it again for a million euros if she tried.

My shillelagh was trembling as I followed the captain into the parlor. The accordion music was deafening now, and I could barely keep my eyes open from the toxic haze.

The Pickle Parlor is a massive venue, larger than a three-ring circus. The floor is a crunchy mix of sawdust, dazed-out leprechauns, lost hats, and old pickle stems. A band of bewitched instruments that play themselves was performing "A Jug of Punch" as loudly as you've ever heard it.

If the music was an assault on the ears, the air was a full-blown war on your eyes. It burned straight to the back of your retinas from a potent mix of three hundred years of hot pickles and a lifetime's worth of leprechaun toots.

I felt like I had descended like Dante into the inferno and that I must turn and run away to somewhere I could breathe—so as not to perish in this abominable, poorly ventilated purgatory. For a moment, I wished that I were back drowning in fastpeat in the Forest of Adair, as it would have been more pleasant.

"Steady, Boyle," said the captain.

I caught my breath and blinked my stinging eyes, try-ing to steady myself. I cleaned my glasses on my jumpsuit.

The venue was an unsavory sight indeed. Of the hundred or so leprechauns scattered around the club, almost nobody had noticed our grand entrance—as all of them were in the midst of the pickle fits or recovering from a hard bonk on the ceiling.

Those few that did notice us blew raspberries or made filthy gestures in our direction. Many of these obscene gestures I had never seen before, so I did not understand how nasty they were intended to be. (*A Field Guide to Rude Leprechaun Gestures* is available in the S&W Department at Collins House or the Joy Vaults gift shop for two euros in paperback, forty-five euros hardcover.)

The only things that definitely did notice our arrival were the three massive woodtrolls* that work the barrelchase.

The barrelchase they were operating is an impressive

---

* Woodtrolls are cousins of bridge trolls that stand upright all the time and have antlers like a stag. They will perform certain kinds of work for gold or treasure without the need for chains.

machine, especially considering it was built in 1723. It's a small roller coaster that takes up more than half of the parlor. Pickle barrels roll a quarter-mile around the track of the barrelchase, spinning, looping the loop—all to keep the pickles inside them awash in their spicy broths. Even while my mind was preoccupied with our case, the idea of taking a ride around the barrelchase did seem like fun for a brief moment.

The largest woodtroll stood about nine feet tall, not counting his antlers. He was wearing a name tag that read MIKEY. Below his name was printed I CARRY NO SHOES. Mikey the Woodtroll approached Captain de Valera menacingly, polishing his large antlers with a filthy, broth-soaked rag.

"Cheers, Mikey," said the captain, as it turns out that they were acquainted.

"Cap'n," said Mikey, nodding his antlers with respect. The next thing that happened was the second strangest thing I would see this day. Mikey and the captain leaned in, and they each took a strong smell of the other's armpit.

Yes. Disgusting. Dis. Gus. Ting. And if you told me I

would ever start doing something like this, I would have called you a filthy, filthy liar. But this custom is called wiftwaffing, and it is the traditional greeting between all manner of trolls. Any greeting other than wiftwaffing between trolls, and somebody gets eaten. This includes all three types of trolls: bridge trolls, woodtrolls, and haretrolls, which are the small kind of trolls that live in underground warrens and are always blind. Haretrolls are also the trolls who will get rid of their bad dreams by putting them into potatoes as they grow underground. If you eat some chips and later have nightmares that you're being chased by a fox, trapped in a dirt tunnel, or being forced to marry a troll that you do not love, you probably ate a potato that grew near a haretroll warren and picked up some of their bad dreams.

"This is Boyle," said the captain, nodding in my direction. "He and I are working a case out of Killarney. Grand larceny. Thirty thousand euros in fine wines."

Mikey leaned in and aggressively sniffed my armpit. The captain's eyes made it clear that I should do the same back to him, and reluctantly I did. Compared to the briny air of the parlor, Mikey the Woodtroll smelled surprisingly not that awful—just a bit like the inside of a barn where friendly chickens have been nesting. One of the best things I ever learned from Captain Siobhán de Valera is to meet the faerie folk with their own customs, and you will get further than trying to impose yours on them.

"Mikey, you wouldn't happen to know if anybody's been bragging about just coming into a vast fortune, would you?" asked the captain.

Mikey chuckled, sharpening his antlers with a small whetstone.

"I just might know the whereabouts of two such rapscallions," he said. "You don't still carry that flask of Jameson whiskey do you, Cap'n?"

Captain de Valera smiled and unclipped the steel flask of whiskey from her belt. She tossed it to Mikey, and he ate the whole flask in one bite, chewing in ecstasy—causing small sparks to shoot out of his mouth.

"Mmm, that's fine Irish steel," he said, munching the

metal flask like a crazy person, or rather the nine-foot-tall woodtroll that he was.

I shot a confused look to the captain, and she shrugged in response as if to say: *Woodtrolls, what are you gonna do?*

It took Mikey a while to swallow the flask; then he cleared his throat and leaned in, tapping his nose conspiratorially.

"If it's Wee Glen and Lovely Liam you're after, they've come in bragging about robbing the beefies, and they've been showing off a vastsack. They've booked out the Rainbow Room for a fortnight," said Mikey.

"You're a good troll, Mikey," said the captain, stretching up and scratching behind his antlers as if he were a puppy. He purred and leaned his head into her hand.

I reached way up and scratched behind his other antler. Captain de Valera and Mikey both gasped and shot me a horrified look, as this was *not* a troll custom, but rather a gesture only performed between very good friends in Tir Na Nog. I had overstepped. The awkward silence would have been deafening if not for the bewitched instruments that were now playing "Zombie" by the Cranberries, and doing a decent job of it.

I pulled my hand away, feeling like the eejit that I almost always feel like in social situations.

Mikey the Woodtroll finally broke the silence and let out a huge belly laugh. The captain laughed, too, and patted me on the back.

"Honest mistake, Boyle," she said. "Just never do it again, because I've nothing to carry your bones back in."

I tried to laugh along just to be part of the team, but I'm sure that with my clenched teeth and my eyes watering from the spicy air I just looked like a jittery teenage pole with glasses and lockjaw who missed being in his shared flat in Galway with Dolores.

"Say nice things about me," laughed Mikey as he turned and loaded a fresh barrel onto the barrelchase. He pointed toward the door to the Rainbow Room in the far depths of the venue.

The Rainbow Room is the private VIP lounge of Bob and Thing's Famous Pickle Parlor, where the pickles are stronger, the ceiling is higher, and the prices are steeper. Lovely Liam and Wee Glen had rented it for a fortnight, which is two weeks. Clearly, they were set on having a picklebender.

We set our positions, and the captain nodded for me to kick the door open, and I must say I felt a wave of excitement. I had never kicked a door open in any type of scenario, and this would be my first one.

Perhaps this is why it took nine tries. Possibly ten. And then, in two-three-more tries after that, oh boy-o—the door broke somewhat in half . . . but enough for us to duck through. Adrenaline flooded my veins. The captain dove through the small opening in the door and rolled into a fighting stance. I tried to do the same but ended up per-forming a belly flop onto the putrid sawdust floor of the Rainbow Room.

Lovely Liam and Wee Glen were right there, puffing their pipes and giggling like eejits on an old sofa, making merry with three of the oldest merrows you have ever seen—these ladies had been out of the water far too long, and it showed.

Merrows are the only faerie folk that technically live in the human Republic of Ireland, as their habitat is the Irish Sea, exclusively. As a result of human misuse and over-fishing, many merrows have had to look for work in the entertainment industry in Tir Na Nog. For a young merrow, say under five hundred years old, there are some opportunities, certainly. But for a middle-aged merrow of seven hundred to a thousand years old—sadly, they may often end up as hostesses in places like Bob and Thing's Famous Pickle Parlor or Johnny Makem's House of Tears and Waffles in Oifigtown, where the famous buttery waffles are custom-made to remind you of a great personal tragedy. Leprechauns are a strange lot.

I did as the captain instructed and focused my eyes like a laser beam at Lovely Liam's shoes instead of at his face. This was not hard to do because his shoes were more beautiful than any person I had ever seen—white silk with velvet ribbons, blue heels, and detailed with thousands of tiny sapphires. The thought that raced through my mind was: *Good heavens, there's a universe of sapphires on his feet.*

Sitting beside Lovely Liam was Wee Glen with the Gorgeous Ears, and his ears looked completely ordinary to me. I couldn't pick them out of a lineup. Indeed, he was missing a finger on his wee left hand. His face looked like a rather bad car crash had happened between a summer squash and a very unhappy billy goat, and this face was the only thing that stumbled out of the burning wreckage.

As it turns out, there would be no time to question either of the suspects, because the moment they saw us, they bolted. Wee Glen's eyes went wide in panic. He started musking, and the smell was of burnt hair mixed with anchovies.

"Beefies—run for the bridge!" shouted Wee Glen.

Lovely Liam tossed a little leather sack to Wee Glen. I can't report Liam's expression because my eyes were fixed on his magnificent shoes, and things were starting to become a blur through my foggy glasses.

"'Twas all his doing! I've no part of it!" said Liam, as the wee folk are quick to throw each other under the coach to save their own skin.

And with that, using his gancanagh powers, Lovely Liam vanished into thin air, or seemed to, by camouflaging himself into the room.

"Curse my eyes!" said Captain de Valera, rubbing them. "Lovely Liam got in my line of sight, and I accidentally looked right at the little devil, Boyle . . . I'm in love. Like my heart has been zapped with Cupid's hot lightning! I WANT TO SHOUT IT FROM THE HIGHEST ROOFTOP. TRUE LOVE! I MUST WRITE A SONG ON ACOUSTIC GUITAR FOR HIM. Now go and catch that gorgeous wee man of my dreams, because I love him so much and must kiss his little head and bathe him in honey!"

This was a disastrous turn of events. After one accidental glance, the captain had fallen madly in love with Lovely Liam. Unfortunately, this is precisely how it works with gancanaghs. She was under his spell, and there was no way to fix it.

"You go for dear darling macushla, and I'll catch Wee Glen!" she yelled.

The captain was in turmoil. *Macushla* is an Irish term of endearment, roughly meaning "pulse of my heart."

Captain Siobhán de Valera was one of the toughest officers I've ever met, but a gancanagh's powers are ferociously strong, and she was fighting to stay professional. I began to swing my shillelagh around the room, hoping to hit Lovely Liam with a lucky shot, as if he were a piñata and I were a blindfolded child who should have taken a nap long ago.

The captain, lovestruck and heart racing, dove for Wee Glen with her leprechaun cuffs, but he was quick with his shillelagh and leveled a firm crack that missed her face but connected with her shoulder.

Captain de Valera rolled backward in pain. Through gritted teeth she growled, "Remind me to make a mixtape for Lovely Liam." This was the first time I had a sense of the captain's age, as I did not know what a mixtape was, but I assumed it was a gift basket of different kinds of tape: electrical, duct, masking, etc.

The captain was in deep, but she managed to fight on with Wee Glen, who took two quick swings at her knees, only to curse when he realized she was wearing knee protectors. The captain got in a good swat and knocked his hat off, which confused and shamed him for a moment.

Wee Glen did a spry flip over her head, landing behind the captain—driving the point of his shillelagh into the small of her back—a cheap shot that knocked her flat onto her jaw.

"I must survive . . . to devote my life . . . to Lovely Liam. I shall make him coupons for foot rubs and brew him soup from only the juiciest rabbits," whispered the captain to me, her eyes filled with wild passion.

Of all the frightening things I had seen this day, watching the captain not in control of herself was perhaps the scariest. It was awful to see her so much in pain and so much in love at one confusing, violent moment.

My fear somehow dissipated, replaced with as much anger as a Ronan Boyle type can muster. I gave up blindly swinging for the Lovely Liam and dove at Wee Glen with a strange growl and a berserk swing of my staff.

I knew that no matter what, I must protect the captain and get her out of this awful den.

My shillelagh took Wee Glen's legs out from under him

and sent him spilling bottom over teakettle across the filthy floor and crashing into the merrows like bowling pins.

The merrows barked and flapped their tails in a panic toward an aquarium across the room. They used their human arms to hoist their fish bottoms back into the water. I wish I had not been distracted by this, for just then, Wee Glen came back at me, twirling his stick like a ninja and landing three fast whacks to my body. The blows were dampened by the cadet jacket, which as you know is Kevlar blend—specifically for striking moments like these.

Now I was as angry as I get—which is pegging a solid seven on a meter that goes to, say, twelve.

I picked myself up and delivered two double-handed swings at Wee Glen. He was faster than me—and good with his staff—but he was also coming out of the pickle fits, and his arms were a foot shorter than mine.

Wee Glen and I whacked back and forth, exchanging strikes at a pace that felt like an old movie running at the wrong speed. I got a few lucky shots in, but I would be lying if I didn't say that Wee Glen was the better shillelagh fighter of the two of us. His whacks were taking a toll—and it didn't help that his stick was made from heavy oak root.

I was no match for Wee Glen. As he landed a hard crack across my temple, I could feel the frames of my glasses snap. I tumbled to the ground, starting to black out.

When I fluttered my eyes open, I couldn't find my glasses, so everything looked a bit like a very scary painting by Claude Monet in his later years.

Captain de Valera was in her love-fever, muttering to herself and scribbling something in her notebook as fast as she could.

"Captain!" I shouted. "Now is not the time. You must fight this feeling and stay strong!"

"I know . . . I know . . ." gasped the captain, trying to finish what she was writing, but it was clear she was losing her inner battle and possibly her very mind. She was two people now, and I didn't seem to know either one of them.

With my vision at about fifty percent, I was plenty surprised when Wee Glen landed on my neck, his shillelagh lined up with my temple as if he were planning to drive my head like a golf ball into the Scottish Highlands. On his shoulder hung the small leather bag that Lovely Liam had tossed to him before he vanished into the scenery.

I did a clumsy backward somersault and shoved Wee Glen off of me. I gave a little kick to his midsection, which caused him to accidentally drop the bag right into my hands and produce a pickle burp that burned off a portion of my eyelashes.

"Careful, it's a vastsack!" called the captain.

This meant nothing, as I did not know what a vastsack was at this time, and I was worried about if eyelashes grow back.

Wee Glen slid across the disgusting floor, kicking up sawdust and stems. He was unaware that this bag of his was now in my hands. I looked into the bag, and I was one second away from learning the nature of a vastsack.

A vastsack is an enchanted bag whose internal compartment is larger on the inside than it appears from the outside. It turns out there are a few of them on display in a trophy case in the astonishingly bad cafeteria at Collins

House. One of those is from the 1800s and looks to be the size of a coin purse from the outside, but on the inside, it is large enough to carry four African elephants. A garda officer in Sligo found this out the hard way when he stopped a clurichaun on a routine ID check, opened the little purse, and dumped four African elephants into his left hand. The elephants were fine, just very surprised to be in Sligo. The officer now has a plastic, robotic hand in the place where he lost that one, and everyone says it's the most interesting thing about him.

Another vastsack I would later see in an evidence locker in the Joy Vaults in Dublin looked like a Dolce & Gabbana Fall Collection 2013 handbag, but inside it could hold the town of Bern, the fifth-largest city in Switzerland.

I was peering into this vastsack like some kind of eejit when the smack of Wee Glen's shillelagh connected with the back of my skull with a dreadful *thunk* that must have pleased him a great deal.

With one of my trademark shrieks, I was sent spinning into darkness that seemed to go on forever. With a soft thump, I landed on an incline of about ninety degrees. If it were a ski slope, it would have been called something like "Widowmaker" or "Big Mistake."

I kept on sliding, trying to get a grip with my hands on the leather wall. I was racing toward who-knows-what at the bottom, and, honestly, running out of shrieks.

That I was now inside the vastsack had not really registered in my brain, as it seemed impossible—the same as it wouldn't seem likely to you that you could fall into your lunch box. The slope started to level out, and about two minutes later, I came to a squishy landing at the bottom of

a pitch-black ravine. I clicked on my torch and tried to get my bearings. I felt like what a genie inside of a bottle might feel like, if the bottle were the size of Wembley Stadium and made of imitation leather.

I screamed out, "Hello? Anybody there?" as you know I tend to say stupid things when I'm nervous. Trying to walk in the vastsack was like navigating a half-deflated bouncy house. I held on to the side and kept my torch pointed ahead of me. Here's what I encountered inside the sack (all entered as evidence at Collins House, in my first case, *People v. Wee Glen*, #770141):

1. An entire herd of stolen sheep (twenty-four in total), their fur spray-painted with a bright pink marking to show that they were the property of a human farmer.

2. One new Mercedes-Benz C-Class sedan with the temporary license plate 7BQ J63 and a parking permit in the window for the town of Claremorris. (Leprechauns cannot drive human cars, but they love fancy things. And they love to steal. And while this is the entry-level Mercedes of a reasonable price, for a leprechaun it's a very

elegant car. I wouldn't be surprised if Wee Glen stole it just for the wonderful smell of the interior.)

3. Four hundred and seventy-five bottles of French wines, the entire former contents of the Malton Hotel's wine cellar. Only four were missing—including a 1971 Petrus. Wee Glen and Lovely Liam drank the most expensive ones first, in classic faerie folk fashion. The concept of "saving something for later" does not exist to the wee folk, and it accounts for about ninety percent of why they get into mischief.

4. A crumpled five-euro note and copious amounts of lint. So much lint that I had to wade through it for some time, up to my waist.

The sheep had surrounded me, and sometimes it was hard to tell where the lint stopped and the sheep began. If anyone could be more nervous and confused than I was right then, it was the twenty-four stolen sheep. They hud-dled around me as I tried to calm my nerves by counting the wine bottles.

I had no plan for how to extricate myself from the vastsack. The walls were too steep to climb without mountaineering gear or leatherworking tools, but this problem would sort itself out a moment later when there was a thunderous shake and I was thrown out of the sack, across the Rainbow Room, and into the disgusting aquarium with the merrows.

The water was frigid salt water to mimic the Irish Sea. Clearly, the tank hadn't been cleaned in ages, as it reeked of algae and merrow poop.

I tried to pull myself from the tank as fast as I could. When underwater, a merrow's eyes cover over with a protective lid that makes them look completely black. It is, in a word, unsettling. Spending even one more second in this creepy tank was not something on my to-do list.

Across the room, Wee Glen and the captain were in a heated stick fight—their struggle for the vastsack had sent it flying and dislodged me from it. A few bottles of wine tumbled out after me, as did one sheep, but luckily the Mercedes did not, as it would certainly have crushed me.

The captain is a master with her staff. She was one of the first pupils of Yogi Hansra. The captain's staff was a blur. It danced from one hand to the other, over her shoulders, behind her back—like the staff itself was alive, and she were some kind of snake charmer taming it. The only way to keep up with the fight was from the sounds of the whacking and the cracking and the *ouch*ing.

The captain was driving Wee Glen backward across the room as I slid down out of the aquarium, wet and shivering, merrow-poop-scented, scanning the filthy floor for my shillelagh or my glasses or both.

"Boyle, catch!" shouted the captain, tossing me her leprechaun cuffs.

I grabbed them out of the air, which was almost impossible with blurred vision. Then she tossed me a crumpled piece of paper, which I did *not* catch. I picked it up off the floor and opened it—it was the note she had been scribbling in a frenzy. It was a short poem.

Captain de Valera shouted to me, "NOW, BOYLE!" as she knocked Wee Glen's staff from his hand and pinned him to the floor, her staff right into his beard. I squinted and read the poem aloud as best I could.

Oh dear little Glen with the most gorgeous ears,
how your beard and your fame have grown over the years.
In Oifigtown square where the traffic's directed,
A statue of you shall one day be erected.
A shining brass Glen, from your toes to your bonnet,
Even pigeons who sit there will not poop upon it.
But lo, how your folly has turned into woe,
As down to the Joy Vaults you're likely to go.
Three to six months of pain, gruel, and toil,
For you've just been handcuffed
. . . by Cadet Ronan Boyle.

And with that, I did clasp the handcuffs onto Wee Glen, as this is the only known method to arrest a leprechaun: lightning-fast moves, combined with a vanity poem. Saying wonderful things in verse about a leprechaun will distract him from literally anything. Wee Glen kicked and fussed, but he was safely in custody. I wish I could say I was a big part of the captain's plan, but my participation was mostly just good luck.

The captain and I caught our breath, feeling quite connected for the first time, as traumatic experiences tend to do that. In the tank, the merrows blank-stared at us with their creepy black eyes. From the main room, the sound of the bewitched instruments could be heard, playing a song by Ragús, the name of which escapes me.

The captain's poem was decent, but honestly, I've read poems by Captain de Valera over the years that knock this one on its bottom. The love-curse had taken a toll, as did the shillelagh fight. Wee Glen wriggled and attempted to make some filthy gestures, but he couldn't escape the cuffs. The captain hoisted him to his feet.

"Nice work, Cadet Boyle," said the captain. "And heavens, you smell truly awful."

I nodded, for the stink of the merrow water in my jumpsuit was dreadful, somehow even here in the Pickle Parlor.

The captain read Wee Glen his rights and picked up his vastsack from the floor, collecting the stray wine bottles into it, remarkably unbroken. I helped corral the loose sheep back in as well, which was a bit of a trick.

The captain tied the vastsack to her belt. I picked up my shillelagh, and we headed out back through the parlor.

"Lovely Liam has disappeared, or is somewhere very near, but we can't see him, which is a shame—for it means our case is not quite closed and that I cannot make him a little crown of flowers, which is all I want to do as I gaze into his eyes, which are the color of a spring sky," said the captain.

The love-curse had not gone away, nor would it until she was treated later that night at Collins House.

We led Wee Glen out past the barrelchase into the main room. Big Mikey nodded his antlers at us as we passed, and many of the pickle-fitting wee folks made more obscene gestures. Someone called out, "Keep them ears shined on the inside, Wee Glen!"

I'm not sure if they meant to keep the inside of his ears shined, or to shine his ears while inside of prison.

We shoved past that thing at the door, which was back on its feet. He put out his hand for a tip, as it's customary to tip the door thing when leaving the Pickle Parlor. Captain

de Valera slipped him two euros, as she is as generous as she is violent.

We loaded Wee Glen into the barrel lift, and I operated the crank that would raise us back up to the street level of Nogbottom. Going up in the lift is much harder, it turns out, and it took us almost fifteen minutes to get back up.

When we arrived at the surface, it was eight P.M., Friday night—because it always is in Nogbottom. My face lit up and I laughed out loud. In all the chaos, I had forgotten that we had left Lily behind. But it wasn't just that I was happy to see her—in her mouth was a strange, wriggling blur.

That blur was Lovely Liam. She had captured him as he tried to flee the scene. He was still camouflaged, but this sort of detail does not matter to a dog. Dogs only use their eyes as a backup sense; their nose is the main way they see the world. Lily recognized his cologne from the Malton Hotel cellar and made the arrest. (To clarify: As the wolf-hounds that work in the Garda Special Unit cannot speak English or Irish or the language of the faerie folk, the policy states that if you are held in the maw of a Special Unit wolfhound, you are automatically under arrest and will have your rights read to you as soon as possible.)

Lovely Liam gave up his camouflage and came into view. The captain stepped forward and kissed him for far longer than was appropriate, but she did manage to get a pair of regular human-sized handcuffs on him. The captain part of her was winning out against the star-crossed lover. Luckily for me, my glasses were smashed somewhere down below in the Rainbow Room, so I can't quite say what Lovely Liam looked like beyond his heavenly shoes, and I did not fall in love.

"Let me go, macushla," whispered Lovely Liam to the captain.

The captain stroked his hair, fawning. It was clear that she was thinking about setting him free. But just then she tightened her grip on his hair, and in one swift move she threw him into the vastsack as she pulled it from her belt.

"And don't trifle with the sheep, my love!" said the captain as she tied the vastsack tight. "Now, Boyle, as I'm a bit beaten up and more in love than I've ever been, perhaps you can lead us home."

I smiled at the captain, and her face lit up. I wouldn't see this again for many months. Pending the presentation of the evidence to a human and faerie magistrate, the Malton Hotel robbery case would be closed. The flock of sheep was a bonus; they had been reported missing from Tullamore. The Mercedes-Benz belonged to a doctor in Claremorris named Frances Gainer, who specializes in freezing the fat off of people's middles.

On the walk back through Nogbottom, I was more relaxed and a bit more confident, which allowed me to take in the wonderful strangeness of the town, even with my hazy eyesight. I noted some of the little details, like the troughs of light beer for the working animals and the ones of strong cider for the nonworking animals.

We passed through the main plaza and headed back toward the Bridge of Riddles. From the apartments high above came the sound of dozens of harps being practiced. A wee leprechaun child, no more than about three hundred years old, waved at me from an upper apartment.

I smiled and waved back, saluting him with my shillelagh.

Then the child called out, "Eat this, ya skinny beefie!" as he threw a rotten cabbage straight at my head.

The cabbage was a direct hit. I would love to tell you that some of this ancient cabbage did not end up in my mouth, but that would be a lie.

I spat and wiped my face as clean as I could, and Captain de Valera patted me on the back.

"Now, Boyle," she said. "Now you truly know what it's like to be one of us."

I managed to laugh at this and wiped the cabbage from my mouth as we started the journey back to Collins House.

CHAPTER TEN

RETURN TO KILLARNEY

n the trip back home, I learned a thing or two.

For starters, the Bridge of Riddles costs three euros and fifty cents going into Nogbottom, but it's fourteen–fifty going out. This is madness. They know they've got you right where they want you. It's like how gum always costs more at the airport. It's not like you're going to use a different Bridge of Riddles. There isn't one. The chubby little far darrig who works the Nogbottom side of the bridge loves to make this joke, saying, "If you don't like our prices, enjoy the competition!"

There is no competition. You either use the Bridge of Riddles or you spend the rest of your days in Nogbottom, eating fake unicorn-and-chips and drowning in tears from the saddest musicals ever performed.

This outgoing rate is not posted anywhere on the bridge, so don't be surprised if you go there and get stuck. The riddle, however, was quite a bit easier on the way out. It went like this:

> *Blind I am, with many eyes*
> *Me da gets mashed, while Mum gets fried.*
> *My brother often,*
> *turns au gratin.*
> *My sister quips,*
> *how oft she's whipped*
> *into a side dish, for heaven's sake*
> *her tots, alas, get boiled and baked.*

If you said "potato," you were exactly right. Although it took me a few moments to think of this answer in my delirious state, perhaps because it was so deceptively easy. The far darrig never even got out of his chair. He just yawned, took a swig off of his ginger beer, and rudely shoved our twenty-nine euros into a pneumatic tube, where it was zipped away.

The trip back through the Forest of Adair took ages. I accidentally stepped too close to a Kissing Colleen sprout, and it took a good little bite of my ankle, which required a medium-sized bandage and some antibiotic ointment back in the medical ward on the fifth floor of Collins House.

An extra annoyance of the trip was that Wee Glen was venting off the last of his pickle toots. He also griped endlessly about the Oifigtown City Hurling Team, saying they were rubbish and wishing a pox upon them.

At my other elbow, the captain would not stop pining for Lovely Liam and singing Ed Sheeran's "Shape of You," which includes the lyric "I'm in love with your body," over and over. This is an uncomfortable thing to hear your superior officer sing, and I tried to get it out of my head. At times, I saw the captain's hand reach for the vastsack, and I could see she was thinking about taking him out.

"I won't really let him go," protested the captain. "I

just want to smell his hair for one second. I'll put him back directly, I promise." I stopped her at each attempt with a swift but not too hard bop to her knuckles from my hemlock shillelagh.

By the time we got to the stream of whiskey, I was so fed up with both of my traveling companions that I let Wee Glen have a long sip from the ninety-proof stream, which made him promptly doze off. I was sick of hearing his nasty opinions about all of the Tir Na Nog hurling teams.*

---

* Hurling is a popular sport in the human Republic of Ireland and even more popular in Tir Na Nog. If you don't know the game, it's as if baseball were played on a soccer field with thick hockey sticks. You might as well call it EVERY SPORT ALL AT ONCE. All of the Tir Na Nog cities have official hurling teams. Lake City Unified combines the three major towns of the Floating Lakes, and it has a stranglehold on the league, with many of the best and most expensive players. The wee folk take their hurling very seriously. Disputes between teams have led to murders, kidnappings, extortion, machine-gunnings, bombings, garrotings, mass poisonings, divorces, stabbings, and even referees being launched out of cannons onto faraway spikes. There have also been more serious offenses that I will not mention here.

If you are ever invited to a Tir Na Nog Hurling League match, DO NOT GO. IT IS NOT SAFE FOR HUMANS. And the unicorn-and-chips are way too expensive. You won't just need protection from the fans but also from the weegees, who rig the league's matches with their trademark corruption and control all of the parking, which is also outrageous.

We passed through the Castleisland geata back into the Republic, and I ineptly drove us back to Collins House. Lily's head was out the window, as was her custom, basking in the afternoon glow of County Kerry. It took us a wee bit to get home, as this was only my second time behind the wheel, and my glasses were shattered somewhere back at Bob and Thing's. The situation was genuinely unsafe, and I grazed a few passing tractors, but the captain was too smitten to care.

Captain de Valera sang the classified song to make Collins House appear, and she did it quite beautifully, as she was still in love, and when you are in love, your voice rings like a spoon against Waterford crystal. She especially nailed the high, tricky part, which I have never quite mastered.

Sergeant O'Brien was at the front desk, muttering and juggling two telephones. She was especially annoyed, as she was between púca forms in her shape-shifting cycle. Currently, her head was a rabbit but her body was a horse, which was a strange sight and obviously made her feel uncomfortable about herself even though it was somewhat beautiful and certainly interesting to see her hold the phones with her floppy ears. When she saw us burst through the front doors, she thrust a hoof toward the Processing Department as if to say: *Don't even ask what kind of day I'm having.*

Captain de Valera entered Wee Glen and Lovely Liam into custody with the help of a trustee troll from the Joy Vaults named Dennis. Wee Glen, still passed out, was stuffed into a muskwrap, which is a humane but smell-proof plastic cling material used to transfer leprechauns in the event of musking.

While Dennis was logging in the sheep, the Mercedes, and the wine, he accidentally glanced at Lovely Liam and fell madly in love. This was especially unfortunate, because when trolls fall in love, they get flushed, sweaty, and ravenously hungry to eat badly behaved human children, and there were none about. It took all of my strength to keep Dennis from devouring the flock of sheep, but by my last

count there were still twenty-three of them, so thank heavens none were lost.

The captain, Dennis, and I were taken into the subbasement for a debriefing session by the staff hypnotist, named the Mysterious Doctor Boiko. The Mysterious Doctor Boiko is *not* a medical doctor, but he *is* a hypnotist from a traveling circus in Romania. He works out of an incense-filled closet in the subbasement. Doctor Boiko was fired from his previous job for "conduct unbecoming a circus." What that is I cannot possibly imagine. He is kept on staff by the Garda Special Unit for situations like the love-curse, when an officer has had a spell cast by the faerie folk that could be dangerous to his or her health and/or job performance. I've known the Mysterious Doctor Boiko for a bit and have been treated by him on three occasions, and even in a building filled with strange things, he is legitimately *very* creepy. The Mysterious Doctor Boiko's mustache connects to his muttonchops in the most circuitous geometry, and he has nine earrings in each earlobe, representing the planets. I know this because they look like the planets. I did not choose to tell him that Pluto is no longer considered a planet, and you wouldn't tell him that either if you gazed into his simmering red eyes that seem to be reflecting a fire that is not there.

I underwent the "Doctor's" hypnosis session, even though I had not actually looked at Lovely Liam directly. This is standard procedure, just to be on the safe side, and while I don't remember the session, I do know that I slept like a baby afterward. It's likely he had served me a Special Unit sandwich called the Irish Goodbye, which was invented in the very active Weapons Laboratory on the third floor of Collins House in 1988.

The Irish Goodbye is a weapons-grade sandwich made with cabbage, spicy Irish mustard, lean corned beef, fear gorta breath, two [CLASSIFIED INGREDIENTS], mayonnaise, and the toenails of woodtrolls on buttered brown bread. Then it's pressed on a panini machine until crispy. The sandwich is basically irresistible. (You can't even taste the toenails, and yes, there is a vegan version.) Almost anyone will take the sandwich when offered, not knowing that it can cause intense short-term memory loss, and it is NOT CLASSIFIED when I tell you that the

Special Unit often uses this sandwich to erase the memory of civilians who have had traumatic run-ins with the faerie folk. If you're wondering why you don't read stories of the wee folk every day on the front page of the newspaper, this military-grade, melt-in-your mouth sandwich is the reason. It's also why all Special Unit vehicles carry a panini press.

I don't recall how I got up to my bunk in the barracks, but that's exactly where I woke up that evening, still in my uniform with a bad case of Irish mustard burps. Someone must have put me in the unreliable lift that I do not like to ride in when I am awake. As a cadet, my bunk was now much closer to the potbelly stove, and Log had once again moved into the one directly next to me. Tim the Medium-Sized Bear was still coming and going on occasion, even though bears have been extinct in Ireland since the last Ice Age.

I told Log all about the trip to Nogbottom, which left her unimpressed—she had been there many times as a young log. She was currently on a case in Westmeath and was sworn not to give anyone any details about it, so she only gave me some.

"Hehehehe," said Log, as she starts most sentences like this. "There's a wee man using rabbit tunnels to traffic stolen credit cards out of Westmeath.* I'm trying to gain the trust of the local rabbits. A whole warren of 'em behind a pub called the Three Jolly Pigeons."

"So, gaining their trust? Are you undercover?" I asked, confused.

"Hehehehehe—no, don't wear a rabbit suit, but I probably could and it would fool them. Rabbits are so, so dim," giggled Log. "They don't even have names, they just call each other 'Kevin'—their mums, das, everybody is a Kevin to them."

"Kevin?"

"Yes, but in the language of the animals 'Kevin' is the word for 'rabbit,' so to them it makes sense."

---

* Credit card fraud is a relatively new crime for the wee folk, but they *love it so much*. You will know the wee folk have compromised your credit card if you've just "bought" a grand pedal harp on eBay that's been mysteriously shipped not to your address but to a post office box in Tralee. One hundred percent of concert-quality harp sales on eBay are fraud, to leprechauns. An entire office of the Special Unit is devoted to fighting this.

Log's psychotic giggle could now get me to fall asleep like the most pleasant lullaby, or maybe I was just more tired than I had ever been in my life.

The following day I volunteered to be on the team to transfer Wee Glen and Lovely Liam to the Joy Vaults in Dublin.

Dermot Lally drove, and somehow he is an even worse driver than me, perhaps because of his dashing eye patch or his main focus being singing along to the radio. Log sat up front with him in the Riot Van, which is a repurposed human vehicle that the Special Unit uses to transfer wee folk. The prisoner compartment has been faerie-proofed and is engraved with thousands of filthy limericks, which the faerie folk love to read and which can keep them occupied for hours. The driver's compartment up front holds six humans and two electric shillelaghs in the event of emergency. Sitting next to me was a nine-foot-tall trustee troll named Carol, who was along in the event that we needed a troll. Carol's nose was blocked up with two small corned beefs, which is standard procedure when traveling with a troll, so that they do not accidentally devour any human children along the way.

Dermot was singing along to Ed Sheeran on the radio as he drummed on the steering wheel. Log joined in with him, even though she did not know the words, she just *Hehehe-hehe*'d her normal psychotic giggle that just happens to fit pretty well with this particular song.

"*Hehehehehe, I'm in love with your body*," they sang, now as a duet. "*Hehehehehe, I'm in love with your body*."

I tugged at my hair. I don't know why, but these lyrics make me very uncomfortable, and everyone I knew seemed to be singing them on a regular basis. I stared out the window, trying to act like I was not with Log and Dermot. Carol was now dead asleep on my lap. Her head was hot and heavy. As we passed through Kildare, I thought I saw a pair of bright red eyes looking right at me as we passed under a bridge. My mind was playing tricks on me. At least I hoped it was.

After the prisoner transfer, we had an hour to spare before we were due to head back to Killarney. Log had been begging to see the wax Liam Neeson on display in Dublin's Wax Museum Plus. While I certainly was *open* to the idea of meeting a wax Liam Neeson, it wasn't as significant to me as, say, a wax Dame Judi Dench would be. And for that, I would have to go all the way to London—trust me, I have planned this hypothetical London trip to see wax Dame Judi in my head many, many times.

So I let Log and Dermot go across the Liffey while I stayed behind at the Joy. I was anxious to see my parents, to make sure they hadn't gotten gang tattoos and to relate to them the story of my bizarre attack at Lord Desmond Dooley's gallery.

I didn't have time to collect falafels, so my parents and I split a Lion Bar that I purchased from the vending machine that rips you off in the visitors' ward. I told Mum and Da of the attack in Dooley's gallery, and the red-eyed wee woman who smelled of fish heads and bit my nose.

"She must be one of Dooley's accomplices," said Da. "He certainly could have had help in stealing the Bog Man. Dooley himself can barely lift a cup of tea."

"Dooley's accomplices are wee folk?" said Mum, shaking her head in disbelief.

"The wee folk are quick and sneaky, and they love crime and a quick profit," I said. "Dooley's in league with this red-eyed woman, possibly others as well. I suspect his crimes go beyond just your case, and further back than we know!"

"Ronan, this is all so much to take in," said Da.

"I know. But Dooley and his little crew are not safe anymore. Now that I'm with the Special Unit!"

My parents beamed with pride; Mum wiped a tear from her eye. I twirled my imaginary shillelagh and pretended to tap my Special Unit badge. This move confused my folks, so I explained what I had just been trying to pantomime.

"Ah, indeed, very good, Ronan," said Da. "Our boy can pantomime with the best of 'em."

"I've started a file on the wee woman," I said, proudly handing over a folder of evidence I had started to collect. Or course, a surly guard blew his whistle and forbade me from actually handing the file to my parents. So I described its contents to them.

The file currently contained three things: a photo of Lord Desmond Dooley that I had downloaded from the Internet; a description of the umbrella that I had lost at his gallery; and my first major break in the case: an almost complete shoe print of the red-eyed wee woman who smelled of fish heads.

"How did you get that, Ronan?" asked Mum.

I said nothing, just lifted my chin to show where the stinky woman had kicked me, hard enough to leave a mark. The impression on my chin was incomplete but close enough to show that it was the symbol of a sheela na gig, a creepy ancient pagan fertility goddess with strange parts. She's said to ward off evil, which in the case of the Red-Eyed Woman the sheela na gig was clearly failing at pretty badly. As no two leprechaun shoes are alike, the print was at least somewhere to start.

My evidence so far was scant, other than Dooley's own admission that my parents were innocent, but who would believe me on that? I stuck the file back into my jacket.

"Bless you, son," said Da. "We're so proud of you."

"I will say, I hope you don't get us out of here too soon," chuckled Mum. "I wouldn't want to miss your father's big night!"

"What now?" I asked.

"Don't be bragging on me, Fiona." Da blushed.

"Tell him!" said Mum.

"Well, you know how I'm in the top gang, the Kinahans, and your mum's in the Hutch Gang?" said Da.

"Yes, and you know I don't approve of this at all," I said sternly.

"Well, I've gotten a little art show organized, showing off the paintings and ceramics of *both* gangs!" said Da proudly. "There's no gap that art cannot bridge!"

"That's grand," I said. "I'm happy for you, Da. Well done."

The guard tapped me, signaling it was time for me to go. I hugged my folks.

Mum hung back and whispered to me. "Good luck, Ronan. And the Hutch Gang is coming to the art show just to rumble. To show the Kinahans who runs this joint."

"To fight? A gang fight? Mum! Does Da know this?" I asked, annoyed.

"He'll be fine. I'll protect him. I'm a pretty big wheel in the Hutch Gang, as I'm the strongest reader *and* typist. I'll look after your da, I promise," said Mum. "I just thought you should know. Love you, boy. Be safe."

I shook my head and headed back to the Riot Van.

On the trip back to Collins House, a very amped-up Log MacDougal told us all about the wax Liam Neeson she had just seen, in greater detail than anybody would ever want.*

My patrols with the captain over the next few days mostly involved misdemeanor cases, one in which the locals up in

---

* Was he taller than you'd expect? *Yes, apparently the wax Liam Neeson is six feet, four inches tall, same as the real-life Liam Neeson.* Did he smell good? *No, he didn't really smell like anything, just a slightly musty smell from the Jedi robes he's wearing.* So he's wearing Jedi robes? Why isn't he dressed as Michael Collins, from the famous film *Michael Collins*? *Well, because they already HAVE a Michael Collins, so a Liam Neeson dressed as Michael Collins would be confusing.*

Guidor thought that their well had become bewitched and was speaking to them directly. In fact, it was a clurichaun at the bottom, trying to convince the townsfolk to throw their coins, pipes, harps, and mobile devices down the well to him. Wee folk have no use for mobile devices, as there is zero roaming coverage in Tir Na Nog, but they do love fancy human items and pretty much anything with the Apple logo on it.

Another case involved a púca who had infiltrated an elementary school on the north side of Dublin. She had taken the form of a fox, which children love and can relate to. In secret, she was teaching the children how to rig the video poker machines in the local pubs. The children were just pawns in this game, and the púca was keeping all of the profits. By the time the captain and I arrested her, she had eleven thousand beer-soaked euros in her tiny fox pants, and she owed the pub owners of the north side of Dublin over three hundred euros in unpaid drinks.

The púca tried to shape-shift into a horse while in

custody in the captain's jeep, but under stress a púca can't choose her form—so she ended up turning into a cat, which Lily easily snapped up and held in her teeth until the transfer was complete.

CHAPTER ELEVEN
A GIFT

round five P.M. I was lying in my bunk in the barracks, writing another postcard to Dame Judi Dench, trying to ignore the ghost of Brian Bean, who had perfected a new impression. "*Tell the coppers you can't catch him*," rapped Brian, his ghostly pants pulled just a bit down to show the top of his ghost underwear.

"Oh, Brian. Wow, so great, that's a new one you've got, then. Brilliant," I said, never looking up but knowing full well from my peripheral vision that he was doing the rapper Lil Wayne.

"*YOUNG MONEY! YOUNG MONEY!*" he continued, not reading the room at all and really going for it.

"Has Log seen this new impression?" I interrupted, knowing that Log was working down in the astonishingly bad cafeteria, and that his going there would send him many floors away from me.

"She has!" said Brian in his ghost voice. "In fact, it was her idea for me to come up here and show you! '*I'M ADDICTED TO SUCCESS!*'" And just like that, he was back in Lil Wayne mode.

I'm not proud to say it, but there are many days that I wish Brian Bean had not died on Frolic Day. When he was alive, you could at least hear his footsteps approaching. In death, he managed to be everywhere, *all the time*. While still somewhat hilarious, he was mostly becoming a bit of a chore, and if I could sense him haunting nearby, I would change my route through the building to avoid having to be the test audience for one of his new bits. His Lil Wayne was amazing, no two ways about it, but luckily I was saved as Lily the wolfhound arrived, nuzzling my shoulder, signaling me with her humongous head to follow her.

Lily's appearance in the barracks was unusual, as the canines of the Special Unit live in and tend to socialize in their own dormitory called Wolfdew on the second floor of Collins House.

Wolfdew has three bay windows that look out onto Lough Leane. The opposite wall is made up of gorgeous mahogany dens stacked up like bunks. Nobody knows where the name Wolfdew came from, but it's likely an abbreviation of the phrase "Wolfhound Dormitory on Two."

There are peat fires that burn twenty-four hours a day in twin stone fireplaces that bookend Wolfdew. There is no cafeteria, as meals are on demand whenever the hounds choose them: smoking rich bowls of roasted lamb with a side of duck, or vice versa, followed by well water and ice creams that are suited to dogs' taste, such as Old Chicken in a Paper Bag by the Train Tracks and Discarded Nachos Near Vagrant's Shoe. Yes, they are very specific flavors, but a dog's nose is one thousand times more advanced than ours, so I understand the need for specificity. I am reluctant to tell you that I have seen Lily devour two entire bowls

of an ice cream called Neighbor's Sweaty Butt After the Gym, which is an enormously popular flavor. They can't keep it on the shelves.

The wall opposite the bay windows has polished oak ramps that lead up to the dens, which are dim and cozy. Each den is lined with sheepskin throws and knit blankets made from the softest wools of the Aran Islands. The name of every wolfhound that has lived in a particular den hangs in order on a brass chain above it, ending with the current resident. Lily's den, for example, starts with a wolfhound named Maude and links down many names to Lily. (Maude was Lily's great-great-grandmother, I would find out, as hounding for the Special Unit is a skill handed down in families.)

Wolfdew is such a cozy place that I half joked with Sergeant O'Brien that I would want to be transferred there out of the human barracks, and she laughed so hard that she pooped some pellets out—she was in her rabbit form at the time, and this can be uncontrollable. Another great lesson Captain de Valera taught me about the faerie folk: Don't judge.

Lily nudged me, and I buttoned my jumpsuit and grabbed my shillelagh, and we trotted down the many flights of stairs to meet Captain de Valera at the porte cochere.

The captain's mismatched eyes were fixed on the fading sky above, and she seemed distressed.

"Except for Tin Whistle, at which you are a disaster, you've done well, Cadet. I had a feeling you would. This is for you, Boyle," she said, tossing me a long package wrapped in brown butcher's paper.

I unwrapped the paper to find a glistening oak-root shillelagh of the first class. It was of a medium thickness, thirty inches long, and with a powerful claw at the head that was carved to look like a small fist. The entire stick clocked in at over seven pounds. I know that detail because I still carry this shillelagh today, and I think my right arm has grown a bit stronger than my left from the carrying of it.

I stood there for a moment, unable to speak, as I was so moved by the gift, which is rare, because I usually blurt out stupid things when I am nervous, and I could have said something ridiculous like "Wowsers!" or "No way!"

Luckily, "Thank you, Captain de Valera" is what I finally blurted out.

"Don't thank me," said the captain. "Your old one is rubbish, and I need you at your best tonight. Reports of a harpy in County Wexford."

With that, she took away my training shillelagh and snapped it in two with remarkable ease, tossing the pieces into a trash can.

I wish I had said a bit more to her right then. Maybe something about how she had changed my life by picking me for the Special Unit. Or perhaps something about how she had become the mentor that I hadn't had since Captain Fearnley. Or I should have said some bit about how she was a much better influence on me than Dolores, or just some stupid thing to tell her how much she meant to me. Not that I . . . loved her? No. That would be silly. But I didn't say anything. Most likely because I held her in such esteem. I just said, "Thank you, Captain de Valera," and left it at that. I would regret this for a long time.

I gave my new shillelagh a few practice swings, until I could feel a glare from Captain de Valera's eyes, indicating that I should follow her.

"Come, Boyle," she said. "We could be in for a long night."

CHAPTER TWELVE

A HARPY IN COUNTY WEXFORD

aptain de Valera gestured out toward the field that runs from the porte cochere all the way down to Lough Leane. I could see nothing particularly out of the ordinary because I was adjusting to my new glasses, which had earlier in the day prompted Dermot Lally to say, "Check out Little Rick, he's so smart now!" Ah well.

Down below there was a slight ripple upon the lake and a bit of mist rolling by in the moonlight. The pungent smell of decomposing lakeweed blew toward us and helped to wake me up a bit, as I had barely slept at all that day. Most of my sleep shift was spent in a nightmare, where I had to fight Yogi Hansra on the middle part of the Eiffel Tower with only the kind of tiny spoon they let you use to taste gelato. Turns out that this dream—induced with help from Doctor Boiko— was actually her very, very surprise final exam. This was unexpected, and having known the yogi for a bit, I should have expected it.

"Don't ask them any questions, and certainly don't say what year it is, as it will upset them," whispered the captain as we crossed the field, our feet mushing in the sod.

Lily growled at something that I could not see yet.

I tested my new shillelagh, uncertain whom, or what, I was about to meet.

I kept my eyes locked on my feet, and I saw that the mush was soaking my cadet boots all the way through. I knew that I would have to dry them by the potbelly stove when I returned, as if this were something to worry about. My next thought was that if I were to leave my boots by the stove, Log would definitely steal them, as she was raised like that and doesn't know any better.

The captain had stopped moving up ahead of me. The lights of Collins House were fading behind us. I could hear the gentle lapping of Lough Leane on its shoreline.

I turned and took a glance back toward the barracks, but as there are no windows up there, I could only see the light from the windows of Wolfdew, which glowed like a sleepy giant. I wished I could be in there, curled up in Lily's den, watching her eat a bowl of Macaroni and Dead Bird Found Near Discarded Man's Swimsuit.

The House itself was starting to fade, as nobody was singing the classified song with the high and tricky middle part to it. A moment later it was just a picnic table again.

Portions of this next passage are classified, so I will tell it as best I can, without compromising my colleagues in the Special Unit, or the faerie folk.

POLITE WARNING!

Portions of this next bit have been edited, as they are still very much classified.

All the best,

Finbar Dowd
Deputy Commissioner
Special Unit of Tir Na Nog

"Wexford is an epic drive," said the captain. "We don't have that sort of time. We have an arrangement to be transported by our faerie allies, per the 1975 accord. Provided that the travel never be for personal or leisure purposes. So brace yourself, and keep your receipts."

"Right, sure." I nodded, shivering. The captain put one hand over my mouth as her other one spun me to face three shining, translucent sylphs.

She covered my mouth so I would not scream out loud and embarrass everybody. This was a good move, as the record-breaking shriek I made did not get very far past her glove.

You may know that a sylph is a flying spirit common to Ireland. True. But the reality is a touch more complicated. There are oodles of flying faeries in Tir Na Nog and the human Republic of Ireland. (There is an entire guide book called *Flying Faeries of the Emerald Isle and How to Kill Them* available in the S&W department at Collins House and the Joy Vaults gift shop for seventy-five euros hardcover or fifty cents in paperback.)

Some of the flying faeries in Ireland are actually Canadian faeries that drifted here, as very light faeries are subject to the Gulf Stream winds, which blow right across the Atlantic Ocean. True story: Moments before the R.M.S. *Titanic* struck an iceberg in the North Atlantic in 1912, Captain Edward Smith had just telegraphed the rest of the North Star Line, saying, "Holy cow, so many faeries floating by me right now. Wow, so neat! Hang on, funny sound downstairs . . . back in two shakes."

There are hundreds of types of airborne faeries, including three kinds that do not mean any harm to humans. Right now, only the sylph concerns us. A sylph is more than just a flying faerie—a sylph is the ghost of a faerie.

Sylphs combine the magical powers of the wee folk with the enhanced powers of the dead. When a faerie dies—which takes millennia, at least—some of them go to the place beyond the northern mountains in Tir Na Nog, and some get stuck behind in the human Republic and become sylphs. Sylphs generally look like the undead version of what they were in life except that you can see right through them, as they have become a collection of electrons. All humans and faeries are basically electrical creatures, so when they die, they leave behind clouds of electromagnetic energy. Ireland is packed with ghosts because the climate is so moist, and water conducts electricity.

You might be wondering, is it fun to get flown around by a sylph? No. Not a bit. Have you ever been to a family reunion, and some aunt who smells like soup and who you haven't seen in ages hugs you too hard because she thinks you're adorable and she hasn't seen you in ages? That's what it feels like when a sylph wraps itself around you, except that the thing that they're hugging is your central nervous system. No person who's ever been flown by a sylph has done it without wetting their pants a little bit.

I am not an exception to that rule, because there are no exceptions.

This first time felt like I was on a scary carnival ride, but the operator could not hear my cries to let me off because he had been murdered. Yes, murdered. This fictional detail to my simile is unnecessary, except that it adds to the horror of the picture I am trying to paint.

It seems I yelled, "*Makeitstopmakeitstopmakeitstop*" on the entire twenty-eight-second ride to Wexford. I know you're thinking, "Ronan Boyle—twenty-eight seconds is not that long, grow some backbone," but at the time my backbone was lit up like the marquee of the Opera Supreme Magnifico, and dry underwear was many hours in my future.

Thirty seconds later, we had been shivering on the coast of Wexford for about two seconds. A thunderstorm was raging, and I shuddered from the pelting on my face while wishing for the fillings in my teeth to cool down, as they had grown very hot from the sylph trip.

I put a note in the mind catalog to bring fresh underwear

next time this happens. Lily was rolling on her back in the rocks, howling like a werewolf. Wolfhounds do not like to travel via sylph because of the high-pitched noise that the electricity makes to their sensitive ears, and the screaming of any terrified humans who are traveling with them can also be quite annoying.

Captain de Valera was calmer than I was. Her jet-black hair had fallen out of its usual bun, as her metal hair clip had melted on the trip. (Some metal items cannot travel by sylph.) She shook her head and let her hair fall over her shoulders. It was longer than I expected, as I had only ever seen it pinned up. Her badge had not evaporated, but it was glowing bright blue with the residual electricity, as were her flasks and buckles.

The captain paid the sylphs with three little bags of tobacco. This was purely a symbolic gesture, as they had no way to use it. They vaporized into the mist, leaving us on the beach that was comprised of approximately a zillion small stones. No Irish beach is ever what you think a "beach" is in your mind's eye, and diving for a volleyball on many of them could be fatal.

An old lighthouse towered over us. This building, called Hook Lighthouse, is somewhat famous. Seems it's been operating on this spot for about eight hundred years.

Two garda with badges from the nearby town of Waterford ran up to us in quite a state. They were the ones who had called in the harpy. Both officers were named Danny by sheer coincidence. They had seen the harpy, and this fact was corroborated by their faces, which were green and horror-stricken, the blood drained out of them. They had multiple bites on their hands and faces, as harpies attack from above, and there's little one can do to fight them off without a strong shillelagh. While harpy bites don't hurt all that much, it's the side effect of the bites that is a serious concern.

Most faerie folk have the right to travel back and forth from Tir Na Nog without a visa. Not harpies. Harpies are heavily restricted. This policy dates back to 1906, when a medical assistant named Marguerite McSheehy at Trinity

College Dublin completed a study of the effects of harpy bites on the human bloodstream.

A harpy looks like a massive crow with the face of a human who unfortunately has the face of a dried-up crab apple. A harpy's wingspan can grow to eleven feet across, greater than a California condor's. Their feet are strong enough to catch and carry a leprechaun or a small human. By day they hang upside down in nests that are made from the stolen stuffed animals of happy human children.

Not too long ago, all of the Irish fishing villages were worried sick over the calendar change that would happen on New Year's Day, March 21, 999. At midnight, they would switch over to AD 1000, and many folks wondered if their sundials would still work, or perhaps the moon might explode, ruining the tides and subsequently killing all the fish. This was obviously a bunch of blarney, but once a mob mentality sets in, it's hard to convince people of anything other than what they want to think.

A fisherman and his wife lived in the tiny hamlet of Tramore, which today is a slightly larger tiny hamlet. At the height of the calendar hysteria, the fisherman caught a magical salmon, almost two hundred pounds in size. The salmon sang with a magnificent voice and offered him a deal if only he would put him back in the sea. (Even today, humans making magical pacts with singing fish account for thirty percent of the workload of the Special Unit.)

Here was the bargain the singing salmon offered: If the fishermen of Tramore were to bring one human child every New Year's Day as a sacrifice, the salmon would make sure their nets were full of delicious fish all year long, in perpetuity. Forever and ever.

The fisherman went home and tried to find a local child who was disliked enough to feed to a large fish with an off-the-charts singing voice. When the local kids heard about the offer, the nasty ones fled, and the sweet ones got their acts together. At the time, Tramore had a pretty nice bunch of kids, and nobody was willing to part with even one of them, let alone a new one every March 21.

One villager came up with a plan to trick the magical fish, and the whole town played along. At the sacrifice ceremony, the villagers wept and keened as they handed over a pink little baby wrapped in his basket. The mother was beside herself. The magical salmon ate the baby, then burped it out whole. The baby hissed and scrambled around the dock and then climbed straight up a pole with his little claws, because of course he was an adult badger that had been shaved and put into a onesie.

The magical fish was not fooled and was, in fact, very annoyed. She also happened to be an evil queen of the merrows named Bébinn. Merrows love to shape-shift. They will turn into singing fish just to test the resolve of humans. Why? I do not know, except that it must get dull down in the depths of the ocean, and according to the World Wildlife Fund, great white sharks eat twelve hundred merrows a year, so they're looking for a bit of fun wherever they can find it.

Bébinn shape-shifted back into her merrow form. She splashed her tail, blinked her black eyes, and swept the entire town up with a huge wave. As the villagers clambered onto their rooftops, she set a curse upon them, saying:

Since ye do not keep your bargains,
A mighty curse upon yer noggins,
Pucker yer lips, kiss your arses goodbye,
From this day on, you'll just have to fly.

And with that, she cursed them with a humongous spell, turning them into the first known flock of harpies. Winged creatures with the faces of crab-apple humans.

Today harpies are flown for sport in the Shousts, which are illegal jousting tournaments in the Undernog. Leprechaun riders fly on them in a thatched-roof coliseum in North Ifreann. Two riders try to knock each other off their harpies with sharp shillelaghs. It's a brutal sport that injures many leprechauns and kills some harpies. Most of the leprechaun riders come from the lower classes, looking to the Shousts as a way to a better life. The harpies are caught in the wild and forced into the Shousts. Many of the harpies who compete are served spicy okra vindaloo before each match, to make them extra-aggressive. Like many parts of the underbelly of Tir Na

Nog, the Shousts are controlled by the wee gaiscíoch, the weegees.

In 1906, McSheehy submitted herself to direct harpy bites for ten days straight in a laboratory. Her notes were meticulous, and they can be read in the library at Trinity College in the bottom of a tuba filled with enchiladas, per her instructions.

This is because harpy bites give you terrible ideas. Ideas that you cannot unthink.

"Bad ideas, Ronan Boyle?" you ask. "What's the big deal? I've heard some bad ideas in my life." Well, I'm talking about the worst ideas you've ever heard.

McSheehy spent the rest of her days trying to make a Volvo-sized cat out of spaghetti that could also be used as a flotation device.

Why? What would this even be? Would you eat it later? Why did it have to float? Why was it the shape of an animal and a car?

No one knows. That's harpy poison.

Everyone around her knew this was a terrible plan and

also pointless. But a human poisoned by a harpy cannot tell the difference between the good and bad notions in her head. McSheehy died, crushed by her own failure and a massive debt to the Barilla pasta company. Also by the force of two tons of dry noodles falling on top of her.

The two garda on the beach who were both named Danny were in quite a state. They dabbed at the cuts to their foreheads, panic in their eyes.

"A huge bird! With the face of a witch with very dry skin!" said the taller Danny.

"Talons like razors. The shrieking . . . like a thousand souls in pain. That's when we called you!" said the rounder Danny.

"Well done, lads. We'll take it from here," said the captain. "Where did you last see the creature?"

"It flew into the lighthouse—and the keeper's in there," said taller Danny. "I, for one, think we should wait and see if the creature turns into butter."

"NO, I'VE GOT IT!" said the rounder Danny. "We take the harpy to London, work on some demos, and get it a deal singing at a major record label. After building up a fan base, playing some shows, she'll be famous!"

"Yes!" interjected the taller Danny, his eyes now insane with the bad ideas of harpy-bite poisoning. "This sounds like a plan! Take the harpy to London, get a record deal, then invest all the money we make into cryptocurrencies!"

"Why did we never think of this before?!" screamed rounder Danny, smacking his own forehead so hard that he knocked himself to the ground.

Since we had traveled by sylph, we were lacking our panini press and could not make these officers an Irish Goodbye sandwich, which would wipe their minds clean of this traumatic incident.

Captain de Valera's hand reached for the smallest flask on her belt. "These lads have some amazing ideas, don't they, Boyle?" she said. "Let's have a toast to celebrate."

"Indeed!" said the rounder Danny, snatching the flask from the captain. "And then let's mail our shoes to Belize. We'll be rich!"

"How?!" I blurted. "That makes no sense whatsoever."

"Now, now, Boyle," said the captain, winking the green one of her two available eyes. "You just don't understand. Let the boys have a drink."

The Dannys laughed, and each tossed back a shot from the flask. A millisecond later, they had collapsed onto the rocky beach. The captain picked up the tiny flask and clipped it back onto her belt.

"Black Anvil. Clurichaun-made whiskey from Oifigtown Harbor, distilled exclusively for the Leprechaun Royal Navy, ten thousand proof. That's five thousand percent alcohol. Illegal almost everywhere since 1800. It gets its name because it's like having an anvil dropped on your head. Don't worry, they'll be awake in four weeks," said the captain.

After a moment, I said the thing we were all thinking.

"There's a leprechaun navy?"

"Yes. Probably the least reliable fighting force in the known world," replied the captain. "The leprechaun navy is basically a heavily armed musical-theater troupe with two boats. Now let's get this bird contained."

From the back of her belt the captain pulled out two

harploons, which is the slang term for a Handheld Harpy-Catching Harpoon Launcher. The device is an explosive cardboard tube about nine inches long. It's packed like a flare and shoots a thin but very strong net that can contain a harpy.

"AWAY WITH YOU, BEAST!" came a shout from the lighthouse. With each pass of the light, I could see a man in silhouette fighting off a winged creature with a wrench. The image would appear, then be lost as the light in the tower spun around.

"We must get to him," said the captain, looking for the door into the lighthouse.

"I think he's going to come to us," I replied, as my new glasses were starting to adjust and I could see that the window was spiderwebbing behind the man.

"I've got him!" I shouted out for no particular reason as I ran.

The lighthouse window exploded above us, and the man tumbled out into the air.

My vague plan was to somehow catch the man, but I

could now see that he was far bigger than me, and this would be like trying to catch a rhino on a lollipop.

But as I had no backup plan, I was going to try.

I arrived at the base of the lighthouse just as the falling keeper arrived from the air. I certainly would have been killed by his velocity if not for the quick thinking of Lily, who knocked us to the ground at just the moment he hit my arms, breaking both of our falls.

I was so happy that I kissed Lily directly on the snout, not even caring that she smelled like a pint of Neighbor's Sweaty Butt.

"Boyle, look out!" shouted the captain.

Above us, a female harpy stretched her wings and howled. The mouth of a harpy is comprised of razor-sharp teeth, and this one still had almost all of hers intact, which is rare, as harpies do not floss. In the raging storm, her wings spanned almost nine feet across. It created a terrifying tableau.

The harpy swooped down and landed on my right arm, knocking me down again. She tried to take a bite out of my midsection. I owe a lot to the cadet jacket and its military-grade lining. While the harpy made contact, she couldn't pierce the material, leaving only several deep bruises around my middle. I swatted her away with a satisfying crack from my shillelagh. She ascended into the rain above us.

The man who had fallen on me was the lighthouse keeper. He had several bites on his arms and face. I picked him up, trying to shield him with my body in case of another swoop.

"Bless you, lad," said the keeper. "If we get out of this mess, I want to take you out to a new restaurant I'm going to open called Let's Go Dutch. It's Dutch food in Dutch ovens served under Dutch paintings."

"Ugh. I mean. Oh. Sure. Sounds fun, brilliant," I replied, trying to hustle the man to safety while the harpy circled in the air above us, regrouping.

He wiped at the bites on his face as he continued his terrible restaurant pitch: "At Let's Go Dutch, you'll smile Vermeer to ear!"

Good Lord, it was awful to hear this idea. And now

puns to go with it. What even is Dutch food? The whole enterprise sounded like a black hole for someone's money.

The captain took off her long leather coat and put it over the shoulders of the keeper, comforting him. She clicked on her torch and waved it in the air, trying to draw the harpy's next attack.

"Get out of here and go and work on this amazing restaurant concept," the captain said to the keeper, as she was out of Black Anvil and we had no panini press.

The dazed keeper nodded and trotted off into the dark, muttering about stroopwafels, which must be some kind of Dutch food.

"Boyle, lure her with your torch, and I'll try to get a shot with the harploon," she said.

"Check," I said, wiping my foggy glasses and clicking on my torch. Unfortunately, I had now lost sight of the harpy in the dark. Thank heavens for Lily, whose nose could not be tricked; she barked at a nearby set of rocks.

I spun my torch and saw the harpy perched right there, ready to pounce, not twenty feet away.

Captain de Valera fired her harploon just as the harpy unfolded her wings. It was a bad shot, as it managed to catch the creature's head and one foot but left the wings completely free. This meant that the harpy could still fly, which she did, pulling the captain into the air with her.

Lily and I gasped as the harpy took off, with the captain dangling and kicking on the other end of the harploon. The captain was towed across the sky.

Lily and I ran after her. Faster than I ever remember running before.

CHAPTER THIRTEEN

BATTLE IN DUNCANNON

y heart was about to explode as we dashed through the fields toward the last spot where we had seen the captain. The night air was setting my lungs on fire. Lily's nose was leading us at this point, as the captain had vanished from sight.

We reached a ridge overlooking Duncannon town. I knew that I had to stop and catch my breath or else I would collapse. Lily, however, is one of the strongest wolfhounds you or anybody has ever seen. She did not need a rest. She nodded for me to climb onto her back, which I did, wrapping my arms around her big strong neck. She took off again after the scent of the captain, barely slowed down by the addition of one Ronan Boyle.

We galloped through the squishy fields until we joined up with the R737 road and made a left into Duncannon. We had lost several minutes in the chase, but hopefully the impairment of the harploon and the weight of the captain had slowed the harpy down a bit. On the R737, Lily picked up a great deal of speed, as her wide paws now had a solid footing. I struggled to hold on, burying my face in her fur.

The town of Duncannon was deserted at this hour. The only sound was the storm. The desolation made it particularly startling when a green carriage cut in front of us, nearly taking my and Lily's heads clean off. The carriage was pulled by a massive black horse. It veered, almost tipping over, and raced on toward the center of town.

"What eejit would be racing around in a carriage at this time of night?" I thought to myself and then said out loud to Lily.

I would not have to wonder about this for long, as just

then a brass shillelagh came out the window of the carriage and was shaken at us, accompanied by a specific filthy leprechaun gesture (see page 74 of *A Field Guide to Filthy Leprechaun Gestures* as a reference).

Someone with a frighteningly familiar face was driving the coach, cracking a long whip. It was the wee woman with a nose that looked like it was put on upside down.

The Red-Eyed Woman from Henrietta Street.

The nose biter. Dooley's accomplice.

"Lily! It's her!" I cried out as I touched the part of my chin that had once held the wee woman's shoe print. Lily growled, even though Lily had never met the Red-Eyed Woman and did not know to whom I was referring. But Lily is so very loyal that details like this didn't matter.

The carriage raced up the hill toward the old fort. In gold print on its side was the coat of arms of the wee gaiscíoch—little warriors—the profoundly corrupt police force of Tir Na Nog. Of course, the Red-Eyed Woman was a weegee. She has precisely the temperament, criminal ethics, nasty smell, and violent manners of a wee gaiscíoch officer. She ticked every box. When she'd poked my eyes at Lord Desmond Dooley's gallery, it was with a brass shillelagh—an illegal weapon carried exclusively by the weegees.

How I was such an eejit to have not put this together before, I do not know.

Whatever the Red-Eyed Woman and her weegee gang were doing in Duncannon at this hour would, without a doubt, fall into the category of major mischief. Where there's smoke, there's fire—and where there's fire, the weegees probably started it to cover up some terrible misdeed or to dispose of a corpse they've left behind.

Seeing the Red-Eyed Woman set me off, and I leaped off of Lily's back and began chasing the carriage at a full sprint. Lily ran behind me as we spilled into the main plaza of the old fortress. The stone fort is walled all around and sits twenty or so feet above the water on a strategic point in the Waterford Bay.

The weegees had arrived ahead of us, and the scene was unnerving. Five leprechaun weegees, four males and the Red-Eyed Woman, had emerged from the carriage.

Captain de Valera had grounded the harpy, who was still half-caught in the net. The harpy was in a panic, attempting to fly and howling.

The captain and the harpy were in a tug-of-war with the harploon net, and I could only hope that the captain had not been bitten. At this point no blood or bites were visible on her.

The weegees had surrounded the captain and the beast. The Red-Eyed Woman was now using her whip on the harpy, which was cruel and disgusting. The weegees had come after the harpy as well—only we were in the Republic of Ireland, and clearly this was our jurisdiction. The weegees had no reason to be operating in Duncannon on a random Tuesday night. Unless they were illegally capturing a harpy to return it to the suffering of the Undernog Shousting tournaments.

My mind flashed back to the large birdcages in Dooley's gallery on Henrietta Street. The strange droppings. It was all starting to add up. If Dooley dealt in stolen treasures and mummies like the Bog Man, why wouldn't he also sell a harpy or two?

"We're just here for the harpy, Boyle. She's worth a thousand heels* in the fighting dome," said the stinky Red-Eyed Woman.

"Let us have the bird, and we'll let you walk away from here with your knees intact," said the Red-Eyed Woman, puffing vigorously on a clay pipe that was slightly longer than her entire body.

On her vest she wore the badge that showed her rank as High Commandant Most Revered of the Wee Gaiscíoch. (The ranks of weegee officers are as ridiculously overblown as leprechaun names. For example, a cadet—the same level that I was at this time in the Special Unit Garda of Tir Na Nog—is called Humongous Admiral Number One in the wee gaiscíoch.)

In my years of dealing with the weegees, I have found that they always start conversations with humans with something along the lines of "How would you like me to mail you and your knees to Dingle in separate boxes?" This is not an idle

---

* Leprechaun slang for money, as fancy shoes are so important to their economy.

threat from a weegee. There is a photo collage in the astonishingly bad cafeteria in Collins House in tribute to three Special Unit officers who actually were mailed to Dingle in boxes separate from their knees by corrupt officers of the wee gaiscíoch. It's a vicious crime, made only more shocking by the fact that the weegees are willing to spend money on postage for two separate boxes. Weegees are as thrifty as they are nefarious. All of those Special Unit officers survived, by the way, as An Post, the Irish postal system, is outstanding, and their knees arrived in Dingle on the same day as their bodies.

Nearby, the captain had pinned the harpy to the ground in the most surprising manner.

"Are you bitten?" I cried out to her.

"I don't think so!"

The captain popped up, spitting out a mouthful of feathers. Captain de Valera was biting the back of the harpy's neck, hard. To subdue a harpy, the only known method is to bite them first. This was discovered by accident in the Joy Vaults in the 1960s when a riot broke out and several strong harpies attacked a clurichaun named Famous Tyrone. His full name was in fact: Famous Tyrone Who Bites His Enemies Without Warning, which, unfortunately, the harpies did not know, as you have to guess the names of wee folk, and this is very time-consuming.

The wee gaiscíoch officers tightened their circle around the captain and the confused, frightened harpy. The weegees were armed to the teeth: brass shillelaghs, cudgels, and spray canisters of military-grade hot pickle juice—which is illegal everywhere in both the human Republic of Ireland and Tir Na Nog.

I had now known Captain Siobhán de Valera for many months, and I had a feeling what would happen next. The captain never waits to see how a situation will unfold. Instead, she strikes first. But as she was currently holding a full-grown harpy at bay with her teeth, I knew that this was my moment to act. It was up to me to fight back with a level of ferocity that would leave our opponents in a state of utter dismay.

Perhaps fate had made Captain de Valera give me the new shillelagh on this exact night so that I could act as her hands in this fight. Or perhaps it was just a lucky coincidence.

I rubbed my frozen fingers and shortened up my grip on the new fighting stick, getting used to its robust weight. Compared to my training staff, this one felt like a small cannon.

I was emotionally and physically wrecked, shivering in underwear that had not been changed since my sylph flight. To top it off, I had not had a decent night's sleep since the time I dozed in Log MacDougal's arms and she sang me songs in the language of the animals.

All of my training—except for Tin Whistle for Beginners—had been leading to a moment like this, where I was cold, outnumbered, and facing five powerful wee folk.

When I saw the Red-Eyed Woman take a swing at Captain de Valera with her brass staff, part of my brain split off from the person I used to be, and I became someone else. Someone different—and honestly, someone scary.

I bared my teeth and howled like a lunatic.

The weegees recoiled in surprise, because if you saw me, you would never expect me to howl like a wild animal.

I leaped and leveled a huge swing at the Red-Eyed Woman's solar plexus. It was a direct hit and sent her flying almost twenty feet into the stone wall of the fortress. The heavier shillelagh packs a huge wallop, it turned out. Her bronze shillelagh skittered across the cobblestones.

All of the weegees started musking. The combination of smells was a nightmare of the highest order. Five leprechauns musking at the same time created the sense that someone had left a poop soufflé to burn in an oven built from octopus parts and rotten teeth.

Before I could get my balance, two of the larger male weegees had wrapped themselves around my legs like bloodthirsty toddlers, trying to topple me over.

Lily's huge mouth clamped down on the head of one of the little men just as he tried to bite my knee. The yelp the little man let out was muffled, as his head was no longer visible. Lily shook him like a rag doll and then flicked his body over the wall, presumably into the bay, or more likely onto the sharp rocks just short of the water. It was impossible to hear what happened in the pounding rain. (Note: Please do not shed any tears for this wee man that Lily tossed over the wall. You could drop a leprechaun from an airplane, and he would get up laughing and then steal your cow. Leprechauns are spry and virtually indestructible.)

The second wee man wrapped on my leg watched Lily's send-off of his comrade, his mouth agape. How he managed to keep his pipe from falling off of his lower lip is a mystery. In his distracted state, he had no time to prepare for an enormous swing that I delivered to his feet—sending him in a backward somersault into the wee-gees' carriage, which jostled, spilling all manner of contraband out of it: leprechaun gold with the stamp of the Royal Mint in Oifigtown, smoking pipes made from unicorn horn, and a dozen of the most magnificent shoes you have ever seen, each with solid platinum buckles. Also, a half-dozen claddagh jars, no doubt filled with the awful secrets of the weegees. There were also several remarkably carved logs in the shape of human children. I had to pick one up to realize it was a log.

Through the driving rain, I could just make out the shape of a human figure inside the carriage, and from his silhouette, I had a good idea who it was.

The Red-Eyed Woman was back on her gorgeous gold shoes, and she did a rather spectacular cartwheel toward me. I took a few swings at her, but she was as quick as a snake. I landed a few sloppy shots—nothing that could do any real damage.

What happened next has given me nightmares many times since. The three remaining male weegees stacked themselves up, one on top of the other. This new "tall" leprechaun rushed at me like a centipede, brandishing three bronze shillelaghs. A dizzying blur of swats and punches from this confusing centipede-thing sent me tumbling across the cobblestones. The Red-Eyed Woman popped up and sprayed me with a short blast of her military-grade pickle juice canister.

It is no mystery why this item was banned by the international organization Human Rights Watch back in 2009. Had I not been wearing my new glasses, I would have been blinded permanently. The glasses saved my eyeballs, although they themselves melted away. The exposed part of my face suffered a hot-pickle burn of the fourth degree, leaving my skin the color of a baboon's behind. The pain was

staggering, as if someone had peeled the top layer of my skin off and gently tucked a colony of fire ants underneath it.

Across the plaza, the captain now had the harpy fully contained in the net. Lily rushed to her side and bit down on the harploon's rope, holding it tight.

The six-handed leprepede lurched toward me. I closed my useless eyes, took a deep breath, and swung at it.

My first swing was such an epic miss that it hurt me more than anybody else. I was not controlling my breath, which is the number one rule of training with Yogi Hansra. My second swing was accompanied by a satisfying *thunk* and a tiny yelp, as the wee man in the middle of the stack went flying. His sudden absence sent the other two tumbling like a bearded house of cards.

I began to spin my shillelagh in front of me, using both hands like an unstable majorette in some kind of angry parade. This proved to be a good tactic, and I made many direct hits with the weegees as they ran at me. I kept pressing forward, spinning my staff until I could hear nothing at all over the whir of the wood.

A downside to fighting an opponent with an illegal brass shillelagh is that whenever you make contact, it hurts your hands, as the reverberations are strong. Especially on a cold night, which Ireland has in spades. So now my baboon-butt face and my hands were both burning, and I had swallowed some of the pickle spray and it was sliding down the back of my throat.

I could just make out the Red-Eyed Woman pulling something off of her belt and waving it toward Lily. I was horrified to see that it was a high-quality French chocolate bonbon, and chocolate is very dangerous for a dog. You know this, and I know this, but dogs cannot remember that they can't have chocolate. Luring Special Unit wolfhounds with chocolate treats is a wicked move, even for the weegees, and it made me angrier than I already was, which was a solid twelve out of a possible fifteen on the Ronan Boyle meter.

"NO!" I shouted as I jumped for the bonbon, my body becoming parallel to the ground. I caught the chocolate in my frozen hand, and then ate it, out of sheer force of habit. It was remarkable.

The Red-Eyed Woman pounced onto my shoulder. Her tiny fist landed several jabs at my nose with a set of brass knuckles that were so beautiful, they belonged in a museum. But the joke was on her, because my face was already so numb from pain that these hits might as well have been kisses from the world's most agreeable Chihuahua.

Lily still had control of the harpy, which freed up Captain de Valera, whose purple shillelagh shot out through the night like an eel. She delivered an astonishing combination of *thwack*s and *bonk*s that were difficult to see with the naked eye and impossible to see with mine.

I pulled myself up, switched my shillelagh to my left hand, and took a huge swing at the Red-Eyed Woman, delivering a wallop to her nose that already looked like it was put on upside down.

I thwacked her two more times across the noggin, knocking her hat off. My confidence was on the rise. Her stinky musk was coming on strong, and it was like we were inside an airplane that was stuck on the runway in which every seat had been purchased by fish heads. I was driving her backward toward the carriage. I was surprised with the ease with which I was gaining advantage over her.

"I haven't forgotten you," I shouted at her as we whacked at each other with our sticks. "You bit my nose at Dooley's. I've got your shoe print. I will have my revenge. Also, I will get my umbrella back, as it's a nice umbrella."

The Red-Eyed Woman cackled, even though she was losing the duel. This should have been a clue. I will never really forgive myself for the next turn of events. My adrenaline was pumping, and it seemed like I was winning, but remember: The wee folk are unrivaled in their devilish cleverness.

I could have acted differently and saved the captain from being stolen away from the Republic on that night. As Yogi Hansra had taught me: The failure of your endeavors is because of your ego. And right now, my ego told me that I was being a real hotshot.

But really, I was about to be duped by a tiny stinky woman with a nose that looks like it was put on upside down.

The Red-Eyed Woman's trick was one of the oldest-in the book. Literally. So literally that it's covered on page three of the course book for *Practices of Irish and Faerie Law*:

Never accept gold from a leprechaun. All leprechaun gold has been mallact.* Which just means a curse has been cast on it. The same way that we can faerie-proof doors against the wee folk, they enchant their gold to keep it from falling into human hands. This is why I've heard of only two cases where a human got off with a pot of leprechaun gold. Those crocks were foolishly left uncursed by their wee owners.

But I wasn't thinking about my Practices of Irish and

---

* There are at least two hundred known mallacts that can protect faerie gold, all of which are catalogued in the pamphlet *The Handling and Safe Storage of Mallact Faerie Gold*, available in the Joy Vaults gift shop in Dublin or the S&W Department at Collins House for two hundred and ninety euros in hardcover or best offer in paperback.

If you accept gold from the wee folk, one of the curses will befall you. Some of them are fast and painless—like going instantly bald, or losing your sense of humor. You will meet men and women who have been a victim of the latter one, as they are always out in droves on election days. Some of the curses are ironic and cruel. I would later read about some mallact gold that made a man named Brian O'Flaherty from the town of Doon have an insatiable desire to eat the gold. He melted it down and stirred it into a Bolognese sauce that looked amazing and tasted not amazing.

Faerie Law class at all, which is why, like the world's biggest eejit, I instinctively put my hand out as the Red-Eyed Woman tossed a gold coin at my face.

Everything slowed down for a moment. I caught a good look at the figure lurking in the carriage, and indeed, I knew his face well. He smiled and winked at me, which felt like adding insult to injury.

I'm certain I meant to slap the gold out of the air, as we had been specifically trained to do at Collins House. But I did not. I was distracted, and I blew it. The gold was now clenched in my stupid fist.

I had accepted leprechaun gold. That's when the nightmare began.

Chapter Fourteen

TO THE UNDERNOG

hen the Duncannon paramedics found me at daybreak, they thought I was dead, because I seemed very much so. My body was paralyzed. Frozen solid, mouth agape, with a piece of heavy gold clenched in my petrified fist. Thank heavens, someone checked for a pulse before they sent me to the morgue, and they were surprised to find that I was very much alive inside my body. I was not aware of my surroundings because of the tromluí. It's a pretty simple

curse: The person who accepts this gold goes to live in a nightmare from their own memory. From the moment I had caught the coin, while my body was in Duncannon Fort, my mind was reliving one of the most embarrassing moments of my short life. Vividly.

Luckily it was my most embarrassing memory, and not my worst memory, for I wouldn't have survived the day of my parents' arrest over and over again.

This was just a humiliating event, and yet to live it over and over was rough indeed. The place was Eyre Square, central Galway. Dolores had introduced me to her pretty cousin Bridget Sullivan, who is a bit older than me and works at Powell's Music Shop. Dolores had rented us Rollerblades for what I realized later was a blind date, because Dolores is a bit crazy and decided that I should try to meet a girl-friend before I turned sixteen and "became boring."

Bridget was nice enough, I supposed. We were attempting to skate around the park, which is difficult, as Eyre Square tends to be full of legitimate kooks.

I thought I would try to impress Bridget by doing a little jump over two small stairs that led from one level of the park down to the next. The entire "jump" would have been about fifty centimeters, had it not resulted in serious bodily harm. Something, perhaps a lace, had caught on the top step as I tried to lift off, and with a horrible crack—which was the sound of both of my wrists breaking—I landed in a split, causing a massive rip in my pants. A pigeon nearby coughed up a pizza crust right as it happened.

I'm not sure if the pigeon was reacting to my fall, or if it was just amazing timing. It certainly added some sad punctuation to the whole affair. I wish I could tell you that I did not start to cry, but if you've never broken both wrists at the same time, trust me—you are going to cry. And I did.

So there I was. Pants split, wrists snapped, near a pigeon with tummy trouble—all from trying to do a "stunt" to impress Dolores's lovely cousin Bridget Sullivan.

Needless to say, I would probably never Rollerblade again.

But now the gold curse was causing me to relive this moment again and again. And again and again and again, while paralyzed, in the wet plaza of Duncannon Fort. While I was in this tromluí state, the Special Unit at Collins House was contacted, and the Mysterious Doctor Boiko was dispatched by sylph to the scene, along with Commissioner of the Special Unit Colm McManus, who is a handsome and somewhat severe man of about sixty who carries a white shillelagh, which is quite rare to see. This kind of shillelagh is made from the root of the hilarity tree, which grows only on the west coast of Tir Na Nog. Hilarity tree is a classic clurichaun name, because the tree is in fact the most poisonous plant in their world. Just one of the hilarity tree's fruits contains enough poison to kill a herd of the most robust hippopotami.

Doctor Boiko brought me out of the tromluí with the aid of a very disgusting tea that is designed for this purpose and must be served directly into the nose.

Duncannon Fort was eerily quiet as I came to. The storm had passed. The captain, Lily, and the Red-Eyed Woman were gone, as was the harpy. At this point I did not know what had befallen them.

"Captain de Valera?" I asked, my voice raspy from a long night of shrieking.

The commissioner shook his head as he consulted a shenanogram that was wavering listlessly. "She didn't report in. Likely that the weegees have taken her. And the wolfhound. There's a few geatas around here; we're checking them all."

I picked myself up. I was angry but also severely

exhausted, still reeling from my pickle-burnt face and now a noseful of a potion that seemed onion-based. I tried to control my breathing, as the yogi had taught me. I'm not sure if I was shaking on the outside or just the inside.

"I'd like to request permission to go and find her, sir," I said.

"You need to rest a bit first, lad. You don't look well at all," replied the commissioner, looking me up and down with genuine concern. His eyes lingered on my baboon-butt face, then turned away, as if he couldn't stand to look at it.

"Of course, sir. I understand. I would need to stop at Collins House first. I require some things from the Supply and Weapons Department. And I need our second-best wolfhound," I said, staring off at Waterford Bay. My eyes, which could not focus, caused me to squint with an intensity that accurately represented the anger brewing inside me.

I wanted the captain back. I wanted Lily back. I feared what terrible things would befall them in the custody of the stinky Red-Eyed Woman.

"I cannot send a cadet into Tir Na Nog to recover a captain, Boyle," said the commissioner.

My heart sank, but my voice strengthened. I stretched tall and grabbed hold of the commissioner's arm, which was both passionate of me and a breach of protocol.

"But it must be me," I pleaded. "They're my friends. And the weegees have an accomplice who is well known to me. I saw him in their carriage. He even winked at me."

The commissioner twirled his white shillelagh. He stared out at the bay. We were now locked in a quiet competition to see which of us could stare at Waterford Bay with more gravitas. After a long moment, he finally turned back to face me.

"The Special Unit does not send agents on vendettas, Mr. Boyle. I'm aware of your parents' legal situation. The stolen Bog Man. I know all about your history with Lord Desmond Dooley, who is a well-connected man. And who, I should remind you, has been found not guilty in the highest courts of the land."

"Yes. I understand. But I have to go, sir. It must be me. Please."

The commissioner furrowed his brow, then tapped me with his white stick, which was as light as a feather. "Let me finish, boy. I cannot send a cadet to Tir Na Nog . . . so I shall have to promote you."

I smiled. Which hurt my face a good deal in its current state.

And that is how, at nine o'clock that night, I set off for my first mission to the Undernog, accompanied by Log MacDougal and a large gray wolfhound named Rí.

My face was tingling, my body bruised, but there was an undeniable spring in my step, for I was wearing a new uniform for the first time—camouflage kilt, kneewhack guards, wool and Kevlar jacket with epaulets. On the left breast, a gold badge bearing a single word that identified my new rank: LORGAIRE, the Irish word for *detective*.

This was my first night as a detective of the Special Unit of Tir Na Nog.

I will tell you now the one detail that I kept from the commissioner. The figure in the weegee's carriage, the one who winked at me. He was well known to me. And his face would haunt me for the rest of my life. But not because it was Lord Desmond Dooley.

Because it was the Bog Man.

ABOUT THE AUTHOR

THOMAS LENNON is a writer and actor from Oak Park, Illinois. He has written and appeared in many films and television shows, as well as the music video for "Weird Al" Yankovic's "Foil." This is his first novel.

ACKNOWLEDGMENTS

Crazy love to Jenny Lennon for her paintings, her passion, her support.

Sniffs to Lilo Bear Lennon, who plays all of the dogs in this book.

Sláinte to Timothy and Kathleen Lennon for taking me to Ireland and forcing me to drive.

Respect to Robert Ben Garant for making me try to keep up with him.

Homage to Peter Hedges for showing me how cool it could be to write every day.

Wink to Craig and Megan Ferguson for taking me into their mysterious cellar.

Go raibh maith agat to Brendan and Marnie Farrell at Turin Castle, County Mayo.

LARGER THAN MEDIUM-SIZED BEAR HUGS TO THE PEOPLE WHO MADE THIS BOOK

Stephanie Rostan, superagent and many-handed remover of unicorns.

Karl Austen, finest attorney of the human realm.

Peter Principato, my wartime consigliere.

My so-smart-it's-actually-scary editor, Maggie Lehrman.

The lovely designer Chad W. Beckerman, who picked out this font for his name.

The hilarious people of Abrams. Fearful reverence to the high-functioning gancanaghs in publicity, weapons, pickles, and discount sheerie flights: Melanie Chang, Hallie Patterson, Nicole Schaefer, Patricia McNamara, and Jenny Choy.

John Hendrix—Stone. Cold. Genius.

With love and thanks to the people of the human Republic of Ireland, especially my grandparents, Michael Lennon of Athlone and Mary Crowe of Hollymount.

To Lennon Wedren for his super reading.

To my sister, Meggan Lennon, for the bop on my soft baby skull that started it all.